SPIDER BABY

A NOVEL BY
DAYNA NOFFKE

BASED ON THE SCREENPLAY BY JACK HILL

Encyclopocalypse Publications
www.encyclopocalypse.com

Foreword
"The Maddest Story Ever Told"
Mike Watt

Screams and moans and bats and bones
Teenage monsters in haunted homes
The ghosts on the stair
The vampires bite
Better beware, there's a full moon tonight

Cannibal spiders creep and crawl
Boys and ghouls having a ball
Frankenstein, Dracula and even the Mummy
Are sure to end up in someone's tummy

Take a fresh rodent, some toadstools and weeds
And an old owl and the young one she breeds
Mix in seven legs of an eight-legged beast
Then you are all set for a cannibal feast

Sit around the fire with the cup of brew
A fiend and a werewolf on each side of you
This cannibal orgy is strange to behold

Mike Watt

*And the maddest story ever told**

In the annals of cult film history, Jack Hill's *Spider Baby* remains unique. Even among Jack's body of work, *Spider Baby* doesn't look or feel like anything else.

Shot like a hardboiled *noir* by Alfred Taylor, *Spider Baby*'s high key photography favors crisp shadows and the dangers within, but the film's tone is straight out of an episode of *The Addams Family*. A laugh track would not have been out-of-place in *Spider Baby*, but by that metric, so would very little else.

Hill was one of those workhorses that are sometimes sniffingly called "craftsmen directors." His father, Roland was a set designer for Warner Brothers, among other studios, his pedigree going back as far as *The Jazz Singer* (1927). Jack attended UCLA with Francis Ford Coppola, and the two of them wound up working for Roger Corman on stuff like *The Terror* and *Wasp Woman*. Read any Corman biography and you'll see the people he put to work in the early years. That's where Jack learned how to "work a budget." *Spider Baby*, for instance, cost a grand total of $65,000, with $2,500 going to Lon Chaney, Jr.

Shot in 1964, the film was shelved when the producers went bankrupt and sat untouched until 1967, when it finally found life on the drive-in and grindhouse circuit. Over the years, it was released—and re-released—under a string of lurid titles, including: *The Liver Eaters, Attack of the Liver Eaters, Cannibal Orgy,* and *The Maddest Story Ever Told*. Chaney passed in 1973. Jack would go on to discover Pam Grier, and drag her and Sid to the Philippines to make exploitation films like *The Big Bird Cage* and *The Big Doll House*. Jack became known as an exploitation king and history supports this designation.

I only met Jack Hill once—he's still with us as of this

---

* Songwriter: Ronald Stein.
  Sung in the film by Lon Chaney, Jr.

writing, so I have high hopes for a second meeting—and mostly we talked about Lenny Bruce, whose daughter, Kitty Bruce, appeared in Hill's *Switchblade Sisters*. I recall him telling me a couple of stories about *Spider Baby*.

(I'm going to try and recreate this thirty-year old conversation from memory.)

"So the loudmouth character, Schlocker, he was played by a guy I met working on… I think it was *Blood Bath*. Karl Schanzer. Kurt worked as a P.I. (private investigator) on the side. While he worked cases, he'd try to get acting work too. Two of his clients were interested in producing a horror movie. It all worked out. But the problem was, I didn't have a script or anything yet."

His primary tale was about adding the "deleted scene" appears as art the end of this book, as a deleted scene. The scene involved the Messenger meeting the Merrye's "normal" neighbors. It was a hastily written scene, as Jack recalled, meant to give actor Mantan Moreland another day's pay. A veteran of vaudeville and minstrel, not to mention close to a hundred films, Moreland's career had slowed by the late '50s. He said that *Spider Baby* was "a weird blessing."

"Plus," Jack said, "it would really be something to see a beloved comedian brutally murdered in the first few minutes of the film. People gasped."

Chaney, too, was grateful for *Spider Baby* to come along when it did. By '64, Chaney was almost uninsurable due to his drinking and health issues. He promised Hill he wouldn't take a single drink during filming. "He kept that promise," Jack said. "And he was prouder of that performance than he was just about anything else."

After that encounter with Hill, I found myself lucky to have gotten to spend a good deal of time with Sid Haig before he passed in 2019. Sid was a great storyteller and he had no trouble holding a room. He loved *Spider Baby*. It was his first large role and he prepared like Hell for it. "I watched animals in the zoo, the way they'd move. Monkeys, yeah, but also the way bigger cats moved. Then I'd go to a playground and watch kids make up stories and run around, pretend to be the animals I'd studied." As Ralph, Sid Haig approached his role with a startling level of depth. He even incorporated elements of Noh theatre into his performance—layering stylized physical expression onto what could have easily been played for grotesque effect. As a result, Haig delivered something strange, sad, and memorable. In every sense, Sid Haig brought something operatic to the role—because Sid was, quite simply, a fucking boss…

As far as this book goes, all hats should be doffed to author Dayna Noffke. From page one she beautifully captures the film's weird tone, its deadpan humor, even its bittersweet ending. Sid would have really liked it.

—Mike Watt (author, *Hot Splices: The Author's Cut*)
April, 2025

SPIDER BABY

Seductive Innocence
of LOLITA
SAVAGE HUNGER
of a Black Widow

Chapter One

Goddamn this heat. The messenger swiped his sweat-slick forehead with the back of a dust-coated hand. *'Bout to melt and become one with the blessed sidewalk.*

The impossibly stout fabric of the messenger's standard-issue khaki delivery uniform of long pants and button down clung to his damp skin. He balanced himself atop a quaking junkyard special motorbike that idled at an unstable *rat-a-tat*, a scorching drumbeat against his thighs. *Enough to put a man's teeth on edge.* He retrieved a dented GI canteen from his saddle bag and tipped it back, his Adam's apple bobbing in time with labored gulps.

The Messenger capped and stowed the canteen, mumbling a few curse words, unintelligible even to himself. He'd long ago made peace with these solo conversations on his delivery runs. Bits of thoughts with nowhere to go. *You're in good company when you're talking to yourself.*

"I am too damn old for this shit...damned heat...shoulda worked for m'father..."

The man tapped an oversized manila envelope against his knee, squinting at the curious address of *Mr. Bruno, % Merrye House.* "Who the hell names a house, any damn way?"

Especially on a road like this. Hippies maybe, he mused. It sounded like something those crusty pink-and-purple shrouded wisps of girls would do. Finding an abandoned house to shack up in with their… *Aw, dammit*. Now, he'd lost his train of thought again. Right of the rails.

There was something *weird* about the winding little road the messenger found himself on, something that had called to him, an impulse to follow, though there was no sign of its terminus. Curiosity had already given way to exhaustion, and even more than that — confusion.

Where is this damn house? The only thing keeping the messenger from turning tail and returning home, his determination waning as he gave himself over to the sense memory of a cold cola: the envelope still staring up at him. *Aw, to hell with it*. As the messenger opened his satchel to stow the parcel the wind caught its corner, sending it skipping off across the dirt, a rectangular tumbleweed.

The messenger let out a mighty heave of a sigh and dismounted, cursing creaky knees as he leaned into the scrubby bushes. He extended his arm and as his hand closed around the crinkled envelope, his eyes settled on something beyond the foliage. He swept back a veil of ivory and vines to reveal a rusting iron gate, the arch of which bore flaked metal etching that read: *MERRYE HOUSE*.

"Merrye house! I'll be hog-tied." The messenger chuckled as he tugged at the dangling bell cord suspended from the column. The rotten thing gave way in his hand, raining shreds of decayed fauna down onto his head. He lifted his riding goggles and peeked through the iron spires.

Merrye House stood, if you could call it standing, a skeleton of a once grand Victorian home. A crumbling edifice of curves and angles, the home's series of windows stared out, like so many eyes, over an empty porch and an expanse of scrubgrass-dotted earth.

The sight of the house and its scorched-earth grounds left

him to wonder *why on earth someone would let a house like this go to pot. That's Hollywood for you. Some real weirdos in there. I'd bet the farm.*

As he stood there, gawking, his nerves pricked to attention, tingling with that undefinable sensation of *something not quite right.*

"Scorcher," he muttered, for no reason other than that he found the sound of his own voice oddly soothing, a sort of tether to reality. He swiped debris from his shoulders and tugged at the gate's iron chain. The disintegrating links gave way in his grasp.

Admitted to the grounds, the messenger biked past the yard's thin-limbed trees, following a barely discernible path, a brittle carpet of fauna and encroaching fungi. Killing the ignition, he called out, "Hey! Hey! Anybody home?"

There was no answer from the flat darkness of the home's many window eyes, which led the man to note how strange it was that a house could appear at one time both deserted and… *what's the word?* "Possessed!" *Like in those creepy, crazy movies.*

He did not linger. Courage, he believed, followed on the heels of an action, rather than the other way around. He tugged at the ancient bell cord, which let loose a dull clunk, and took a step back, shaky hands flipping the letter between his fingers.

To the silence that was the response, he called out, "You don't have to tell me twice!" and turned his back to the house, rehearsing the speech he intended to give his boss: *I tried. I knocked on the door and rang the bell and I'm telling you, there wasn't anyone there. Or if they were, they sure weren't wanting to come talk to me.*

As his foot hit the first step, a sound, a sort of mechanical thud, caught his attention. *Maybe it was the deadbolt,* he thought.

But the door didn't open, and further, there it was again, that creaky thudding. His head turned, a matter of instinct standing in opposition to his own better judgment, toward the source, an open window at the far edge of the porch. Curiosity overtaking him, he scooted toward the sound, pressing his back into the porch rail.

He arrived at the open window, his tired eyes narrowed in an attempt to adjust to the dark interior of the room beyond. It was a parlor, filled as it was with *Great Gatsby*-esque castoff furniture, worn velvets and oiled woods coated in the dusty film of neglect. He noted that the windows to his right and left were identical in size, sealed off from the outside world with swaths of sickly yellow velvet.

The entire thing creeped him out. It reminded him of a film he'd seen, one of those bloody Dracula knockoffs he'd caught at a bargain matinee. Standing as he was at what felt like the summer home of a non-canon vampire, he made up his mind at long last. *Screw this. I'm going home.* He turned on his heel, only to be stopped by the unmistakable *click-thud* of footsteps. He hearkened to it, drawn to that damn open window, to the house's mysterious inner sanctum beyond...

"Hello?"

His eyes were too fatigued to make any sense of what he saw, the terrible incongruity of a child-like figure skipping toward the room from the shadowy foyer beyond. Beyond reason, he poked his head further into the open window.

"Hell—"

His greeting died in his throat, cut off by the sudden violent drop of the window frame! The sash landed on him, a dull guillotine that clamped down on him just below the shoulders. He thrashed his legs, body pinned in the vise of the window sash.

As the window pushed the last of his breath from his body, two thoughts competed for attention: First, that he'd *never have that cold cola*. Second, god had a mighty strange way of ushering folks into the great beyond, given that *this* was the last his eyes would see:

Rushing toward him was an evil vision in a moldering flapper dress, skip-skipping along with two butcher knives raised up high in the shape of an x. A young girl, maybe ten or eleven, with a skip-bounce in her Mary Jane steps and the curly tendrils of hair that framed her wide eyes. She clipped the blade edges against each other, delighting in their metallic clang.

The messenger's senses deadened, his hand unclenched, dropping the sweat-ringed envelope to the floor. The girl giggled, a piercing sound, at the sight of the man's centipedian wriggling.

The edges of his vision having fallen into a softened blackness, he did not see the girl, who was not ten but a guileless nineteen, getting ever closer. The blade tips of her gleaming knives were draped in fine lacy material, which the girl twisted about the messenger's head to the tune of her gleeful shrieks.

"Hahaha! I caught you! I caught you! I caught a big fat bug right in my spiderweb! I'm a big spider and now I get to give you a big old sting."

The last thing the Messenger heard was the whoosh-thump of his beating heart, his throat constricted beyond the ability to scream. He felt a brief rush of warmth as the blood exited his body, leaving behind a cold and blessed silence.

Chapter Two

A shape. Virginia was a shape. Or so she liked to think of herself. She was a shape that emerged from shadows, the dress about her transparent and blighted. She was a lithe, white-draped wraith, just *like those girls in the vampire films!*

She passed her pale hand over the flame of a candle, back and forth, back and forth, to watch the shadows play across the meshy gather of her sleeves.

"A vampire…" she whispered into the quiet. *Vampire!* The thought sent her reeling. One giggle gave way to another, then a fit of them, lifting her from the melancholy of the dark parlor. She'd spent the day reclining there, the heat an oppressive weight on both body and soul. She hated these long days when Bruno was gone, his absence confining her to the house.

She rested her dirty feet on the polished oak coffee table, refusing to remove them despite sister Elizabeth's insistence that she would be in *big trouble* when Bruno and brother, Ralph, got home. Virginia replied to her sister's haughty threats with a thrust of her tongue.

What should I care? She thought. After all, Bruno had alighted to town with Ralph, refusing to bow to Virginia's entreaties to bring her along. Now, she was stuck in the company of perpetually sour *stick-in-the-mud*, Elizabeth.

The Messenger's call of "Anybody home?" was music to her ears, sweet relief from the heat, the boredom, and the loneliness. Virginia's ears pricked up at the sound of a strange voice and she jumped off to skip towards its source, ignoring Elizabeth's warnings about *big trouble*.

The man called out again, his voice a bass boom that urged Virginia toward it, a beacon. Virginia tuned out Elizabeth's admonitions, a low buzz in the back of her mind. "I'm just going to see who is here. I'll just bet he might like to play…"

"You'd better not!" Elizabeth's voice sing songs through the house. Virginia stopped long enough to stick her tongue out, not caring that she was in the other room and Elizabeth could not see her, nor that if she did, the two would end up on the floor in one of their regular hair pull and slap fight tussles.

"S'cuse me! Anybody home?" Virginia paused at the doorway of the grand living room, nerves aflame with the tingly pull of anticipation. Her eyes wandered to the ancient roll top desk in the corner. "Winifred!" she whispered. She looked from the desk to the hallway beyond, the source of the visitor's braying calls.

Virginia slid open the roll top, reaching inside and —

"VIRGINIA!" Elizabeth's head popped into the doorway. Virginia snapped her arms behind her back, hiding the butcher knives, standing at attention.

"Whatcha got?" Elizabeth asked. Virginia smiled through her tightly shut lips. "If you play *Spider* with that man, you're going to be in big trouble. And I won't help." Elizabeth narrowed her eyes, pulling herself into the room.

Virginia held the knives in one hand and straightened her dress with the other. She jumped at the sound of the window's sash, falling hard and fast and landing with a heavy *thud*. She quickly recovered herself, a quiver of excitement snaking through her body.

"Spider, spider!" she cried, as she burst out, into the hallway and on to the parlor, with her two knives raised in front of her. She crossed them, the shape of spindly spider pincers. She loved the echoing cling, metal-on-metal as she sawed them back and forth against each other.

Her face lit up at the sight of her new playmate, exclaiming, "Oh! A delivery man!"

The man's eyes were dark and lifeless, his body folded in half. Caught in the cage of the wooden window sash, he sucked in tiny gasps of breath through a string of spittle.

Virginia's shoulders slumped, a momentary twinge of sympathy riding the nerves up and down her spine. This feeling aggravated her in a way that she could not articulate. She only knew that, whatever this was that she was feeling, she *did not like it.* "Poor little bug." Virginia inched closer to The Messenger, eyes locked on his quivering, jerking limbs.

She watched the man's hand quiver and jerk. "You're just like a big wriggly old centipede, aren't you?" The shine in the man's eyes was dulling fast. Virginia had seen this before; if she wanted to play with him, she'd better start the game now!

She stepped back, a skip-skip and a bow before she spread her knives wide. Strung across the glistening tips was a string of fine lacy fabric, a white covering that shrouded her body from the knives to the floor.

She criss crossed the knives, sawing back and forth in front of her face — *cling, cling, cling* — as she danced toward him.

"Bug, bug, bug!" she sang, winding the lacy web about The messenger's head and shoulders, "I caught you! I caught you!" Virginia admired her handiwork. "Haha! I caught you! I got a big fat bug right in my spiderweb. I'm a spider and I get to give you a big sting!"

The messenger drew what little air he could, the sudden shocking violence of his situation breaking through the fear-paralysis. But now, Virginia's limpid eyes, wide with excitement hovered mere inches from his terrified face, reflected in the shiny metal of her knives.

His shriek was barely a whistle, his useless hands clenched and unclenched. Virginia lifted the knives up over her head. Higher. Higher! Near her jaws, like spiders' *chelicerae*. She click-clacked them together, moving every closer and — with a last shrieking giggle — reared back then whipped the knives downward.

They rose and fell. Once. Twice. Again and again, her arms worked the knives like windmill blades, turning in time to her shrieking giggles and cries of, "Sting! Sting! Sting!"

The messenger watched it all through a veil of blood, his wriggling — mercifully — little more than the confused, dying shocks of adrenaline coursing through nerves and muscle. His hands clawing tight at the window frame, fell limp as Virginia hacked and slashed, his blood spattered and pooled.

The messenger's severed ear fell to the floor, eliciting yet another bloodlusting shriek from Virginia. "Sting! Sting!"

Folded nearly in half, the messenger's body kicked a few more times before it settled in the frame, his neck a tangle of sinew and raw meat. The stream of blood issuing from his throat drained away, slowed to a trickle.

Virginia's bloodlust sated, she stopped to admire the object of her violence. She swiped a wet sleeve across her blood-slick face. "VIRGINIA!" The girl wheeled around to face her sister, Elizabeth, who stood in the doorway, hands on her hips, an officious smirk painted across her features.

"Virginia! Are you crazy? Look what you've done."

Virginia turned to the body, reeling back as if in sudden shock at what she had done. Still, she was not afraid — surprised perhaps, and even a little... proud. She tilted her head to examine the Messenger, moving in closer, entranced at the way the meat peeled away from the bone. It reminded her of nothing so much as the ribs that Bruno prepared for their birthday dinners.

Elizabeth's screech roused her from her trance. "Virginia, are you crazy? Now, look what you've done. You're bad. BAD! Bruno is going to hate you."

Virginia flinched at the word *BRUNO*. She swallowed down her shame, the possibility of his impending anger — *no, he won't be angry, he'll be disappointed. Which is worse*, she thought.

She glanced down at the knives in her hands, the blood drying to a thick crust, and flung them aside.The knives cast away, she turned her eyes, dark with malice, toward her sister.

"What are we going to do now?" Elizabeth spat.

Chapter Three

Bruno's white-gloved hands gripped the polished steering wheel. His stomach flipped, its rumbling growing in urgency as he turned onto the pockmarked road to Merrye House. He gulped, attempting to push down that too-familiar feeling — a trepidation laced with guilt — that he got every time he returned home.

Thoughts collided, vying for his attention. *Perhaps I shouldn't have left the children at home alone... who knows what trouble they've gotten into... What choice did I have? I have to take Ralphie to town and better to deal with one of them then all three... Oh, it's fine. I'm sure it's fine.*

He said it out loud for good measure. "I'm sure it's fine. Almost there, Ralph."

Bruno raised a gloved hand to rest it on the seat beside him. Another hand, this one smaller, curled in slightly like that of an ape — slunk up to rest atop Bruno's. The owner of said hand, a hunched figure curled into the shadows of the floorboard, issued a grunt. The high-pitched sound seemed to satisfy Bruno, who squeezed the apeish hand.

"Yes, Ralph. Almost home. I certainly hope your sisters haven't gotten up to too much trouble while we were gone."

Bruno adjusted his driving goggles and his livery cap, a nervous habit. The ball of anxiety in his stomach roiled at the sight of the turnoff to the rutted road that led to Merrye House.

Bruno squinted at the iron gate ahead, an odd-shaped object stationed off to the side of the columns. He couldn't quite make it out, but something told him it wasn't good.

He pulled the Duesenberg limo to a stop and let go of the small hand. The floorboard figure's desperate hoot received no reply from Bruno, who had already set the brake and stumbled out of the vehicle and toward the shape, which had revealed itself to be the messenger's scooter.

Bruno paled with alarm at the sight of the abandoned scooter and the wide open gate. He spread the doors wider, enough to admit the limo through. He opened the door to get in but a quick glance toward the house convinced him otherwise.

He could see the two girls, Elizabeth and Virginia, out front in their neatly-pressed outfits, wide smiles plastered across their countenances. Virginia jumped rope beside Elizabeth, who pointed to the car. Bruno recognized Elizabeth's expression: that smugly satisfied grin of anticipation that she got wore when Virginia had committed a punishment-worthy offense.

I knew it, I knew it. Oh, what have I done? What have THEY done?

"It's all right, Ralphie. I'm sure it'll be fine," he said, more to reassure himself than the contorted man-child curled in the womb of the floorboard.

Virginia dropped her jump rope to dash to the car. She clapped her hands with delight, her freshly-donned flapper dress bouncing in time with her excited skip. "Ralphie, Ralphie, Ralphie!" she shouted.

Bruno struggled to keep his spiraling worry at bay, as panic inched up his chest. He stopped the car and opened his door, ignoring Virginia's wild performance to call out to her sister, who stood, pursed lips, hands on hips, at the bottom of the porch steps.

"Eizabeth! Elizabeth!" Virginia's voice carried across the yard, a loud sing-song version of "Itsy Bitsy Spider," as she pulled open the passenger door.

A curled hand emerged from the car, followed by two bare feet. The figure, a stooped boy, squatted down in the grass beside Virginia who bent down beside him. Ralphie blinked, rapid-fire, at the sudden onslaught of sunshine.

"Oh, Ralphie!" Virginia put her hands on the boy's cheeks and squeezed, causing Ralphie to first giggle, then squirm from her grasp, skittering across the dusty yard on all fours.

Virginia crawled after him, fingers wiggling in mock threat. "I'm gonna get you, Ralphie!" Ralphie stooped down and scratched his bald head before springing into the brush to hide.

Ignoring the pair, Bruno's voice cracked, hoarse with stress as he limped, a creaking arthritic gait, toward Elizabeth. He grabbed hold of her arms, a bit too hard he quickly realized. She only stared ahead, that smirk spreading wider still. "Elizabeth, what has happened?"

Bruno's willed himself to calm, straightening his pressed livery jacket. *This kind of panic does not become me*, he thought. *The children* —always calling them the children, even as their teenaged years slipped further behind them — the *children require a firm but steady hand.*

There is a certain way to handle them; they do not understand things the same way we do owing to their peculiar and unfortunate malady. Bruno dropped his arms to his side and patted Elizabeth's shoulder. "Now, Elizabeth. You're the oldest and you must tell me what has happened."

The girl opened her mouth at long last. "Virginia did something."

Elizabeth's smirk peeled back from her teeth into a full smile. She cast a sidelong glance, sharp as a pointing finger, at Virginia. "Bruno. Virginia has just hurt somebody real bad. You ought to hate her!"

Behind her, Virginia paused her game of hide-and-seek with

Ralph to stick her tongue out at Elizabeth. Bruno's kind eyes caught hers, a guilty glance that sent his panic tingling again.

"Now, Elizabeth. How many times have I told you that it's not nice to hate?"

But he'd barely gotten the sentence out before he noticed… at first just a speck in the corner of his eye… then, he turned his head to see. Something was hanging from beneath the window at the opposite side of the porch. "Oh no. Oh no oh no!"

Bruno raced past Elizabeth, who stood guard with her satisfied grin, while Virgina hid herself in the shadows of the house.

Bruno stopped, mouth agape in horror. Flies already encircled the messenger's head, buzzing lazily. Bruno shut his eyes, disgusted. He talked through clenched teeth. "One day! I leave you alone for just one day and this is what happens!"

Elizabeth, who had rushed to his side, bent down close, poking a curious finger at the dead man's shoulder. She giggled at the strangely rubbery feel of his skin.

Bruno spun to face her. "One day!" He turned on her in anger but, at the sight of her confused face, softening to tenderness. He lowered his voice. "Elizabeth. I left you in charge. I trusted you… you know that I have to take Ralphie to the doctor in town."

Elizabeth pulled back from the dead body, arms crossed, pouting. "It's not my fault. I told her not too and she did it anyway. She was playing *Spider* again!" She stomped her foot for emphasis. "You should hate her."

Bruno shook his head. "No, Elizabeth. You are the responsible one. You were in charge."

Virginia peeked out from behind a tree to cast a triumphant sneer at Elizabeth, but Bruno took notice and raised his finger to her. He marched down the porch stair. "Virginia! You come over here right this minute!"

Virginia pointedly ignored Bruno's advance. "Ralphie! Ralphie!" she called, giving chase once more.

Bruno sighed, watching Virginia disappear in the tangle of dead branches that passed for shrubbery. He watched Ralph and Virginia roam together amongst the weeds and fungi, all smiles once more. The anger drained from his face, he shook his head and closed the car door.

Ralph let out a screech of joy that sounded something like a cross between a grunt and a giggle. Bruno motioned, beckoning him and Virginia to join his approach to the porch under Elizabeth's reproachful stair. Virginia dropped her head, shame painted across her features and took Ralph's hand. They followed after Bruno up the porch steps.

Ralph, half-stooped beside much taller Virginia, grew excited as they approached the door. He leapt to the railing, his head whipping over to take in the sight that greeted them at the open window. His eyes went impossibly wide with infantile wonderment. "Ohhhhhhhhh."

Yet, even Ralph sensed that this meant trouble and glanced back to Virginia who, cornered between the door and the messenger's limp remains, stood unable to ignore the evidence of her naughtiness. She cast her eyes about, desperate for an escape route but Bruno would give her no quarter.

You have to have a firm hand and let these children know what is expected of them, or risk hastening their decline. Yes, they are ill which is no fault of their own but there is no excuse for not maintaining some modicum of civility.

"Virginia. You sit down right there," Bruno said, guiding her by the shoulders. "You sit there, Elizabeth."

Elizabeth obeyed, as she usually did, but not out of any sense of guilt, for the evidence of her belief in her own correctness was plainly written on her face.

"Now," Bruno said. "You must both listen to me very carefully." The girls nodded solemnly. Bruno paused to gather his thoughts. He didn't hold much hope for getting through to them; it was a losing battle that had slowly worn away at him through the years of the childrens' decline. "You remember last time... when those two children climbed over the wall and Viriginia caught them in her spiderweb. Well, that got people to wondering about us! And that's bad."

Bruno threw a sidelong glance toward the window, fighting back a rising tide of noxious bile. Ralph had removed the messenger's cap and plopped atop his own head. He offered Bruno a wide smile.

Focus, Bruno. Focus... Bruno turned his attention back to the girls. "You know that sometimes Ralph has to go to see the doctor in the city. Like today... and I can't be here all the time. You were supposed to mind your sister and not play spider. Now, you are never, ever, to play *Spider* again!"

Virginia let out a gasp and broke into tears, at not just the prospect of losing her favorite pastime of *Spider* but the disappointment in Bruno's tone.

"You're going to have to take down all of your spiderwebs!"

Virginia threw her arms around Bruno, and sobbed high-pitched cries into his shoulder. Bruno struggled to maintain his stern composure in the face of her anguish.

"Please don't hate me Bruno! I didn't mean to be bad."

Oh, damnit. They just don't know any better, Bruno reminded himself.

Bruno's shoulders dropped and he pulled away to offer a reassuring smile as Virginia continued to pour out her apology. "I'm sorry! I'm sorry. Please don't hate me!"

Elizabeth sat in her smugness. "I told you so."

Bruno ignored her and enfolded both of them in a warm embrace. "There, there, Virginia. Of course I don't hate you."

Elizabeth turned on him. "But you should! She —" But Elizabeth was cut short, distracted by Ralph, who lumbered over to crouch by her shoulder. He turned a damp manila envelope over in his hands.

"What have you got there, Ralph?" Bruno asked.

"Something that man had," Elizabeth replied.

"Hand it here, Ralph." Bruno motioned to him.

Ralph, sensing the imminent loss of his new plaything, hopped back to the window, squatting near the buzzing spiral of flies.

"Ralph!" Bruno, who had less patience for Ralph than the girls if he was truthful with himself, stood and marched to the window and snatched the envelope from the boy's curled hand. He glanced at the unfamiliar address, his heart skipping a beat at the word ESQUIRE. He tore open the envelope and pulled out a sheaf of papers covered in fine print.

The girls ran to him, drawn by the worried look on Bruno's face. "Oh no. This is from a lawyer," he said.

Virginia and Elizabeth stared over his shoulders, moving their lips as if reading the text, which in reality, appeared to them as no different than the hieroglyphs they had seen at a museum back when they were able to go out in public. "What is it, Bruno?"

"What is it?" They buzzed about him, their words colliding into each other. "It's bad, isn't it?"

"Are we in trouble, Bruno?"

"Girls, girls. Just let me read!"

"It's bad, isn't it?" Elizabeth asks again.

Bruno thumbed through the papers. "Elizabeth, just because something isn't good doesn't mean it's bad."

Virginia wailed, "It must be something very bad!"

"Nothing is very bad," Bruno answers, though it was immediately clear that it was indeed something *very bad*. Bruno's hand shook. He dropped the papers, his face going gray then white. He rested his hand atop his chest as if to steady the thudding rush of his heart.

"He's going to come here. *Here*! With other people!"

Ralph hooted.

Virginia shot Bruno a serious look. "Daddy wouldn't like that! What other people?"

"It says that… they want to be appointed legal guardians… as the only other known surviving heirs of the estate of Titus W.

Merrye…" Bruno flipped through the papers, desperate to find something that would clear this confusion. *This can't be right. It cannot be… OH NO.*

"It says that they're coming on the fourteenth of… oh no. That's today!" Bruno consulted his watch, his eyes darting from it to the body that dangled from the window.

Though he would have later denied it, it was in that moment he thought for the first time about running away. *I could leave these children behind. I've done all I can,* he thought. But the idea was fleeting, and when he looked up into Virginia's wide eyes, his thoughts turned instead towards improvising a plan.

"Now children, we are going to have to keep some secrets today. There will be some strange people coming to the house. Pretty soon I'm going to have to go to town to meet them and bring them back here."

Elizabeth shook her head. "No, Bruno. What if they wanted to take us? Can't we hide?"

Bruno took Elizabeth's hand, a show of reassurance. "We can't hide this time, Elizabeth. You'll all have to be very strong."

Virginia's eyes were alight with excitement. "I want to see them! We will have company!" She clapped her hands together.

"Oh, Virginia. You have to promise me now. Promise that you will be a good girl and do as I say."

Virginia, who'd grown to hate the slightest hint of sadness or worse, disappointment, on Bruno's face, seized on the chance to redeem herself. "Yes! Of course I will."

"Can't we just hide?" asked Elizabeth.

Virginia jumped up. "I want to see them! I promise I'll be good." She threw in a deep, off-kilter curtsy for good measure.

Bruno's face betrayed his wariness but he fought that sickening fear down to smile warmly at Virginia. "I know you will, Virginia. And I'll take care of you, just like I promised your daddy I would. I'll take care of all of you… no matter what…" The unspoken thought caused him to pale and turn away, unable to revolve the vision that the thought evoked. He forced himself to look at the window. The sight of the body sent that sickeningly sweet bile swirling in his stomach. "We better get... cleaned up."

Bruno rolled up his sleeves and grabbed hold of the rail to pull himself up. His creaking joints served only to deepen his fear, a reminder of the gravity of his promise to care for the children *until...* He shook his head to clear the thought away and turned, officious, to the girls. "Get the bucket, girls! Ralph, you come with me."

* * *

Virginia's bare feet slid beneath soft waves of suds to the sound of her giggles. She sloshed a dirty mop back and forth, slinging blood-tinged water in every direction. Elizabeth motioned to her to lift the mop and squeezed it out over a bucket.

Virginia turned her head toward the roll top desk in the corner of the room and, having lost interest in the task at hand, dropped the mop.

"Virginia!" Elizabeth cried and took up the mopping mantle. But Virginia was already otherwise engaged, having rolled down the creaky desktop to withdraw a small wooden box. She turned her back to Elizabeth, to hide what she was doing, and she slid open the box's carved door, surprised at its emptiness.

Elizabeth wrung out the mop and stopped to yell at Virginia. "What do you want that for? Put it back!"

Virginia snapped the box shut and returned it to the desk. "Elizabeth, you should hurry up! I want to go and watch Uncle Ned."

Elizabeth slammed the mop down into the bucket, sending yet more pink water splashing around them. "You're not supposed to!"

Virginia marched to Elizabeth and wrestled the mop away. She swung the stick in a circle, narrowly missing Virginia and knocking over the mop bucket. Elizabeth screeched and lunged to grab hold of the mop handle, pushing back at Virginia with it. Just as Virginia fell screeching to the floor, Bruno's voice boomed out from the doorway.

"Girls! Put the mop down. I'll finish! You promised to be good."

The chastened girls dropped their heads and flanked Bruno, landing light kisses on his cheeks as they fled the room. Bruno regarded the mess with disgust, but as was his duty, he mopped.

Chapter Four

Beside the pantry, a gaping square, a crypt-like door, guarded the way to the dumbwaiter shaft beyond. To the side of it, a shadow fell into view. A great hunchbacked figure moved with the lurching gait of a classic movie monster.

Step.

Scrape.

Step.

Scrape.

Bruno limped, his back bent with the weight of the load on his shoulders, a corpse shrouded in oilcloth and trussed with rope. He paused to catch his breath then continued lurching toward the dumbwaiter.

He clamped his hand on the frame of the shaft, leaning in to take the pressure off his aching back. Bruno twisted around so that the body slid off his shoulders.

It did not land squarely, forcing Bruno to bend errant limbs into the shape of the waiter. With the bundle in place, he operated the apparatus's creaky hand crank, sending the platform down. He leaned in to listen for the *thud* that signaled it reached the bottom.

His muscles aching, swollen with the effort, he leaned back

against the wall. His eyes shut, the exhaustion overtaking him; he could have slept right there at that wall but for the sound. That awful, awful sound that echoed from the emptiness below. To Bruno it had always sounded like scuffling, like a restless reptile writhing in its cage.

"No rest for the wicked." Bruno cupped his hands to his mouth and called down to the darkness. "I'm coming Uncle Ned!" He turned back into the dining room and took up an oil lamp from the table.

Chapter Five

Unghhhuh. No thoughts, only sound. An endless moan that haunted and scraped at the inside of his brain. The sound belonged to him, yet he could not stop his lips from twisting to let loose the pain in the only possible way. Had he the capacity for understanding, he may have realized that it was not so much a sound as a vibration, a gnawing attached to his ever-growing hunger.

Uncle Ned and Aunt Clara were *always hungry.*

The door to the basement crept open, revealing a silhouetted figure on the top step.

Uncle Ned rose, a Herculean effort, to drag and adjust his twisted limbs and jutting ribs into the vague shape of an upright human being. He blinked at the beam of light far above.

"Unghuh. Uggggggg," he called out by way of greeting, kicking absently at the pile of flesh beside him.

The shape was a woman, more or less human — more than Ned at any rate. Her flesh had gone dusty gray. Her spindly fingers clawed at the dirt floor, the tips of them having peeled back to reveal chipped bone. Auntie Clara, thrust a foot at Ned to show her displeasure but her lips curled into a skull's smile when she saw what the man was dragging down the steps.

Uncle Ned sniffed at the air, nostrils flaring, the rotting bits of his gray matter firing alight with the only recognizable thought or feeling left within them — HUNGER.

The woman grabbed onto Ned's leg, her fingerbones tracing a bloody trail as she clawed herself up the a standing position. The pair tilted their heads, noses pointed upward, the better to take in the smell of fresh meat.

Bruno limped and sputtered his way down, panting with the weight of the trussed up package. "Uncle Ned, Aunt Clara, I brought you some dinner."

The pair's watery eyes stared up through the square opening of their pit. Bruno reached the edge of the pit and now his smiling face loomed over them. "A special treat. Now don't get used to it. We can't make this a habit after all, but it is fresh and I know how you enjoy it."

Unghhhh. Bruuunooo. A flash of recognition shot through Ned's neurons, and was gone just as quickly. These bits of memory came to him less and less frequently each year, replaced by the swirling darkness that cradled his all-consuming hunger.

Despite his plain disgust, Bruno untied the trussed package and laid it bare to reveal the hastily hacked remains of the messenger. He drew a deep breath and set to work. He yanked at the right hand to free it from bits of sinew and gristle. It was grisly work, and when it finally separated, it was with such force that it sent Bruno flying backward to the floor.

Bruno righted himself and chucked the limb down into the darkness. Uncle Ned and Aunt Clara fell on it, a tangled heap of flesh and bone. They tore into the hand, gnashing into the meet and at each other, fat glistening on their swollen lips.

Bruno turned his head away from the cannibal orgy below and set back to work, this time wrenching at the cartilage of the messenger's shoulder socket. He twisted the arm in circles, but progress was slow and he did not think he could bear to hear those gluttonous sounds — *oh, the sound!* — for much longer.

"*Ahhnnnnnnng,*" Ned called up to Bruno, his blood-crusted hands winding and twisting upward, greedy for *more, more, more.*

Thoroughly unnerved, Bruno gave up on the venture. He heaved the body, first onto its side — *Oh, dear god, forgive me,* he thought — and then gave it a final push into the pit.

With that, he turned on his heel, threw his hands over his ears and ascended the stairs, mumbling a mantra. "I promised I would take care of them. No matter what."

Chapter Six

Hurtgen Forest, Germany. 1944

"INCOMING! GET DOWN!"

Titus Merrye ducked behind a burlap sandbag, pulling Bruno with him. Once a striking figure, his sandy blonde hair the stuff of teen dreams, Titus had become what most men do in war — a hollow husk housing raw nerves and a desperate will to live. Yet his desire to save his own skin was not at the expense of his dearest friend.

More than once, he pulled the young Bruno to the ground, to save him from the fire that rained around them, that had incinerated a young man in the spot Bruno had occupied moments before.

In the pressure cooker of the battlefield, the men grew to depend upon each other in ways that others could never understand — would never *want* to understand. Between moments of terror, time was spent writing letters — Bruno to friends, Titus to his children — both of them growing ever more weary of war and retreating further into their own respective inner worlds.

But Bruno sensed something else weighed on Titus,

something wholly unrelated to the war. Titus seemed to be slipping away, losing track of time and memory. He repeated things, told Bruno the same stories over and over, ended them every time with a horsey laugh that devolved into childlike giggles. His once-voracious appetite for reading all but disappeared and Bruno once caught him fashioning a fake gun from sticks wrapped in lengths of gore-soaked bandage.

It worried Bruno enough to bring his friend's diminishing faculties to the attention of the medic, who promptly diagnosed the problem as shell-shock. Titus was summarily ordered to pack his kit. When he cornered his friend, Bruno would later remember a kind of clarity settling in Titus' eyes that he had not seen in many months.

Titus wrapped his stick fingers around Bruno's wrist. Putting his mouth inches from Bruno's ear, he whispered, "Promise me you will take care of them. I am ill. You must take care of the children, no matter what."

When Bruno insisted that he would, after he found the solid footing of home, it only urged Titus to grab onto him harder, hissing, "Promise me! There is no one else to care for them."

Titus pushed a yellowing photo into his hand— a somber portrait of three children, two girls and a boy, pressed and pleated in their Sunday best. Bruno's reservation faded away, replaced by a mixture of guilt and determination.

Bruno tucked the picture away and placed a steadying hand on Titus's shoulder. "I promise," Bruno said.

And he meant it.

Titus was promptly bundled into a makeshift straitjacket and hauled off on a stretcher, wild-eyed and laughing all the way to the waiting jeep.

Chapter Seven

A cat prowled the weedy afternoon shadows, pausing, suddenly on alert.

Bruno sweated and panted, his shirtsleeves rolled up to hide the gore that stained them. He paused to look at Ralph, who sat in the grass, criss-cross-applesauce, watching the cat.

Bruno paused to wipe his brow and leaned against a tree, drawing in deep breaths while that mantra that had come to define his later years as caretaker to a gaggle of primordial monsters, ran laps through his brain. *I promise. I promise. I promise to take care of them no matter what.*

The "no matter what" clause brought tears to his eyes, as it seemed that might be arriving sooner rather than later.

Still, he had to finish the job at hand, so he rolled *the messenger's* scooter down into the deep ditch to the right of the iron gates. It went down easily but its handlebars would be a dead giveaway to anyone stopping outside the property.

He took up his shovel and set to work, covering the machine with dirt and compost, pausing once to check his watch. Ralph scooted across the lawn to kick a few leaves into the pile. Bruno offered him a pat of reassurance and waved him off. "Go and play, Ralph." Ralph did not move. "Go on!"

Ralph frowned, then scooted away with his swinging squat-walk, stationing himself near the porch steps. He busied himself with a blade of dry grass, turning it in his hand and rolling it between his fingers before shoved the grass deep into his maw, crying out at the taste of blood on his balled fist. Disappointed by Bruno's lack of response, Ralph scanned the yard to find other entertainment.

Suddenly, his head swiveled, eyes locked on the graceful shape of the cat. The cat's frightened movements stirred something in him, a familiar ache, a vibration of sorts that he recognized only as hunger. Unable to control himself, Ralph pounced, bouncing forward on the balls of his feet.

The cat froze, back arched, a statue. It seemed to sense Ralph's desperation. It drew back from him slowly, arching its back, then leapt off like a shot, and disappeared into the weeds, leaving the hungry boy-man behind.

Chapter Eight

Down the street, a girl crawled on all fours in the dirt, peeking beneath bushes and around corners, calling out, "Fluffy! Here, Fluffy." Her eyes were puffy and red, her case of pinkeye worsened by the flow of gooey tears streaming down her cheeks.

The boy kicked his deflated soccer ball toward his sister, barely missing her head, causing her to jump to her feet and give chase. The boy stopped several feet from her to turn and scream, "That old cat probably got hit by a car anyway!"

The mother turned away from the flowers she was cutting, intending to throw the children her patented *you're-gonna-get-it* look, but instead she dropped the garden shears and dashed into the rutted street to yank her terrified daughter out of the way of an oncoming automobile.

The mother swatted the errant child with one hand, shaking her fist at the driver with the other. The chastened girl dropped her head in mock-guilt while her mother spat expletives at the long-gone car. She crossed her fingers — both hands! — behind her back, eyes squeezed shut in prayer that her mother would turn to see her brother, who stood a mere foot behind her, imitating her tirade.

When the mother tired of her rant, she swatted the girl's behind and, in a single movement of remarkable skill, swung around to lay one on the boy as well. The girl couldn't hide her delight and skipped off to resume the hunt for her cat.

* * *

Peter's hand dug into the rubbery leather interior of the car door. "Emily, perhaps you should slow down just a —" Peter gasped in terror as Emily swerved the car wildly to the right to avoid the small child in the rutted road.

"EMILY! My god!"

"Damn rugrats!" Emily said. She reached up to adjust the *oh-so-perfectly* arranged silk

scarf draped about her head and tied in a neat bow beneath her chin. The scarf served as the last defense between her coiffed very-blond curls and the oven that was the outside air.

Peter's neck craned toward the back of the convertible sports bar, his eyes locked on the ever-smaller figure of the girl. He turned back to Emily. "Really, Emily!"

"Peter, if you don't like the way I drive, you may certainly feel free to take a trolley."

"Now, look here. This wasn't my idea at all," he retorted. "You know, the more I think about it the more distasteful it seems. I —"

"Of course it wasn't your idea. You don't have ideas, Brother Dear."

Peter opened his mouth to respond but, *oh, what's the point?* He'd dealt with his "sister dear" all his life and knew better than anyone that she would get the last word. He slunk down into the seat to stare out the window. He figured that, although the silent treatment was unlikely to elicit any response from her, it would at least allow him a modicum of peace.

Peter squinted at a blocky shape in the distance. As he looked to Emily, trying to assess whether she had plans to stop before they crashed into the iron gate flanked by brick columns, Emily skidded to a dramatic stop.

The car lurched forward, sending Peter sliding across the bench seat to slam into his sister, who shoved him off with a gloved hand and clucked her tongue at the unkempt state of the columns.

Peter blinked his eyes, his head still swimming with the whiplash of the ride. "Emily, what on earth makes you think that this is the right place?"

Further in, the house stared out with darkened window-eyes. Foreboding. There was nothing welcoming about the home — indeed, no sign that anyone might live there.

Emily thrust her finger in Peter's face to point at a sign, partially obscured by the dead brush that had choked its way around the columns. "Why, this has got to be it. Don't you see the sign? Right there! It says Merrye Estate."

Peter gulped. "Oh, yes. I guess this is then." He ran his fingers through his windblown hair.

"Don't just sit there, Peter. Go and open the gate."

"Hmm," Peter said. "Oh yes, of course."

He jumped out of the car and stepped forward to — "Ouch!" he cried as his foot gave out from under him, his ankle wrenching to the side on the uneven ground. He withdrew his foot from the offending leaf pile to examine it.

Emily tapped her fingertips impatiently on the dashboard. "Go on, brother!"

Peter waved her away. He took his time looking over his ankle, which had stopped throbbing almost immediately, merely to annoy his sister. He grabbed onto the left side of the iron gate with both hands and yanked it toward him. It gave way with an echoey creak. He opened the other side of the gate and wiped his hands together, shaking off the powdery rust.

"Must you make every task such a production?" Emily asked as Peter slid back into his seat.

"Just drive, Emily." Peter replied.

Peter leaned his head out the window as they approached. Seeing that there was no discernible driveway, she parked beneath the shadow of a small grove of skeletal trees. As the car died to a stop, the two of them took in the full sight of the property's scrubby, unkempt yard.

Peter grabbed for Emily's wrist as she reached to open the car door. "Well hold on, now. I don't see any sign of that… what the hell was his name? That lawyer? Maybe we should wait."

Emily replied, her tone heavy with contempt. "Obviously, he hasn't arrived yet. The caretaker here probably went to the station with his horse and buggy, or whatever it is that they use here. Now come on."

"You go on ahead, Emily. I believe I'll wait for the others."

"What's the matter, Peter? Chicken?"

"I just don't think it's right to go crashing in on someone you're about to sue. It feels a bit…"

"Don't forget why we're here. We hope to avoid that expense if possible."

Emily stared Peter down; it was clear that she expected him to acquiesce, but when he did not, she threw open the door and stomped over the torched landscape to the sagging porch steps of Merrye House.

She stared up at the edifice, at the turret that rose above the encroaching desolation like the arms of a dying soul reaching up.

Emily was impressed with the place. *It might be a little run down but I'll bet it's worth a pretty penny with a new coat of paint — and probably filled with antiques to boot!*

She paused at the door to retie her scarf and smoothed out the curl that had escaped the fabric to rest on her forehead. She tugged on the bell cord over her head; it released a solid, deep clang. Emily rocked on her heels, waiting for a reply. When none came, she huffed loudly and pulled her hand back to knock on the door. Again, there was no answer.

"Oh, this is ridiculous."

Emily knocked again, hard enough to send flakes of paint and rot raining down. "Ugh!"

From the comfort of the car, Peter covered his mouth in an attempt to hide his chuckle of satisfaction. Emily eyed Peter with disdain. It was then that she noticed the open window at the far end of the porch. She marched toward it, calling out, "Hello? Hello? Are you home? Answer the door!"

Emily shouted into the darkness. "Hello?!"

When there was no reply, she leaned in over the windowsill, her body half in, half out of the house, unknowingly recreating the unfortunate messenger's earlier visit. She cleared her throat in preparation to call out again, when a shadow crossed the beam of light bisecting the room.

She recoiled at the surprise, withdrawing from the window just in time to escape the falling window sash! It struck the sill with a booming thud, a terrible force closing off the dark room beyond. Turning she gasped yet again.

Ralph's quivering face hung just a few feet from hers, its quivering lips and owlish black eyes traced her face down to her bosom. He extended his hand in a strange sort of up and down handshake. His mouth opened and closed like a fish out of water, only to release a series of animalistic clicks and moans.

Emily choked out a quick, "Peter!" as she backed up into the porch railing and toppled over.

Peter leapt out of the car, running toward her with his arms open wide. She ran past him and jumped into the car, slamming the door shut. "Emily, good lord. Why are —?"

Emily drew her jacket tighter around herself and shuddered. "Don't be funny. There's an animal up there on the porch. Some kind of baboon or something."

Peter could not help but be bemused. "Well, let's not have a complete double-duck fit!"

"Oh, you shut up!" Emily slunk down into the seat with her arms crossed as Ralph squat hopped down the porch steps toward them.

Chapter Nine

As the sports car passed the slower Dusseldorf, Emily threw an angry glance at the wrought iron monster. Bruno didn't acknowledge the driver or her wound up vehicle. He kept his eyes trained on the bump road ahead, gloves stationed at 10 and 2.

Behind him, and behind the thick glass partition designed to separate a driver from those of higher station, a bubbly young woman, Anne, in a Jackie O-style gray suit, sat alongside a pudgy bulldog of a lawyer, aptly named Schlocker.

Even Bruno, who could be counted upon to conduct himself with the utmost dignity, had to choke down a chuckle when the decidedly greasy man had stuck his hand out and announced his name in introduction.

A cigar dangling from his thin lips, Schlocker struggled with the window blinds which, despite his best efforts, kept snapping up, spinning in desperate circles.

Anne considered helping him — it made her near nauseous to watch him sweat and huff like that — but she thought better of it and averted her eyes to her own window.

Schlocker reached across her lap to flip the blind on her side of the car, his cigar dropping ash into her lap. The woman merely sighed, brushing the dirty powder away absently, as if used to it.

The car lurched to a stop and Bruno rolled his window down a bit to survey the scene ahead. A work crew was out in full force with a flagman waving cars to halt and move as necessary. Bruno quickly rolled the window back up, coughing at the influx of road dust.

The bass booms of the crew's work drowned out whatever Schlocker was yelling — which was probably for the best. Bruno did not even register the empty hum of words until he heard Schlocker banging on the glass partition.

Bruno dipped his hand down below the dash to lift up a long rubber tube with a mouthpiece. He turned his head, motioning Schlocker to pick up his end, which he did only after much cursing and fumbling.

Schlocker eyed the moldy old thing with disdain. He tapped the glass and yelled, "It's broken! I say, it's broken!" Bruno shrugged and pointed once more to the tube. Schlocker fumed. "I don't know what is wrong with this man. Why can't he see that —?" His words dropped off into a dull mumble of cursing.

Bruno nodded, as if he understood the problem and motioned his hand toward the door and then in a circle, then remained in dignified silence while Schlocker grew increasingly frustrated.

Unable to contain herself, Anne broke her silence. She pointed to Schlocker's door. "I think he means the handle is on the inside."

"What handle?" His face was drenched in a sweat that was fast working its way down toward his collar.

Anne calmly leaned forward and lightly tapped the glass. "The partition. The handle for the partition."

Schlocker looked to his door and cranked the handle, winding the partition down. Satisfied that he had solved the puzzle, he sat back. "Yes, yes. So it is," he mumbled to Anne, then to Bruno: "What's going on here? We're stopped!"

"Yes, we are sir. You are correct. They're blasting up ahead, sir."

The limo shuddered with the shock of a nearby explosion. Schlocker's teeth clamped down, truncating his cigar. The front half fell to the floor and the lawyer stamped at it, grinding ashes into the burn hole in the upholstery beneath his feet. "What's all this about? Blasting what?"

"Blasting, sir. For the new highway." Bruno watched the falling rocks with a sad sort of fascination, the one thought circling in his head. *No matter what.* "It won't last long, Mr. Shucker."

Schlocker leaned back, shaken and flung the rest of the mutilated cigar away. "*Schlocker*. The name is Schlocker, Mr. Bruno!"

"Oh, please, sir. It's just Bruno… just plain Bruno."

"I see. Well, all right, Bruno. I want to tell you I appreciate your cooperation in all this. Frankly I wasn't expecting it."

"Cooperation, sir? I don't understand."

Schlocker looked uncomfortable, but for a new reason. "I may as well tell you, Bruno. I was fully prepared to avail myself of the services of a Marshal, should it be necessary. Thanks to your cooperation, it isn't. Well, I appreciate that. I'll certainly do my best to see that it's not forgotten."

"Forgotten, sir?"

"Yes, in the disposition of the property, you know. I firmly believe that so many years of faithful service, no matter how ill-advised, should not be forgotten."

"Thank you sir." Bruno let out a long, worried breath as another boom rocked the limousine.

Schlocker withdrew an engraved case from the breast of his suit. He lit another smelly cigar and made a show of signaling Anne to take out her steno pad. "Now, Bruno. I'd like to ask you a few questions, if you don't mind."

"Why, certainly, sir."

"My understanding is that for some years now, you have been the sole – ah – custodian of the three children of that late Titus W. Merrye. Is that correct?"

"Oh, yes sir. For some years now. It's been an honor to care for the children."

Schlocker, clearly pleased at what he considered to be his great skill in gaining Bruno's naive cooperation, winked at Anne, who took careful shorthand. "And that these same three children have never been allowed the benefits of any sort of formal schooling, is that correct, Bruno?"

"Absolutely not, sir. The master never would have allowed them to be exposed to the other children. In consideration of their... condition."

"And they have not received any kind of professional medical care?"

Bruno was shocked by the accusation. "Quite to the contrary on that score, I can assure you. In fact there have been regular and frequent visits to —"

"You mean they're not well?"

"Well enough, sir. But you see, they're not... ordinary... children."

"I'm sure we'd all agree to that Bruno. Nevertheless —"

"They're sort of... well, different."

"Well, I shouldn't wonder. Nearly full grown, with never so much as a day of school."

Bruno gripped the wheel in his own discomfort. "I don't think you quite understand, Mr.

Schlocker. They have a sort of... it's an inherited condition. It affects their personality, their understanding. It affects their appetites and the ways they can eat. It's very complex, sir, as you can imagine and they require a certain kind of care that I have grown to understand through the years. You see —"

"Now, now. Here, here. I understand all that. But what you

don't seem to understand, my good man, is that there are properly qualified institutions for the care of the... deprived, and those with such unfortunate maladies. Especially when there are substantial properties to be administered. Frankly, I must say I find the situation rather shocking. And may I point out that the law, thank goodness, provides judicial remedies for such abuses. I will have to see the children to judge of course, but I am inclined to think that depriving them of the proper care in such an institution may be considered — well, you'll excuse me, but legally at least — neglect." Schlocker waved his hand at Anne, mumbling at her to "get this all down," even as it was abundantly clear that she had recorded every word of the conversation.

Schlocker's words washed over Bruno without registering. Bruno only stared straight ahead, eyes misting over. The blasting crew's flagman approached the car and signaled him to roll down the window.

A cloud of dust preceded the flagman, who leaned in through the window. "Come on, mister. Let's get this heap moving already!" When Bruno did not respond, the man tapped the dashboard, stirring the driver to action. "I said, get a move on. You're backing everything up."

Bruno returned to the present. "Oh. Yes, of course."

As the limo lurched and bounced back into gear, Schlocker cranked the partition back up. He leaned over, *soto* to Anne — as *soto* as Schlocker's voice could get. "Miss Morse? You understand the import of this information?"

Anne smiled wide, as one smiles at a child to whom she has repeated the same answer hundreds of times. "Yes, I've got it all down, Mr. Schlocker. Every word from 'I understand that for some years, you have been the guardian,' and so forth." Schlocker smiled and patted her knee, Anne instinctively recoiled from his touch.

The limo turned down the lane that Merrye House occupied.

Dayna Noffke

The little girl down the lane was still engaged in the hunt for her kitty in a neighboring yard, while her brother was just as engaged in torturing her by following her and yelling, "I bet your cat is dead!" As the limo passed them, the boy chucked a handful of rocks at it.

Chapter Ten

While Emily had busied herself with first fixing her makeup and then simply sinking down into the driver's seat for a good, long sulk, Peter went exploring. The boy-ape that had frightened Emily must have been in turn scared away by her shriek, and had long since disappeared, perhaps into the dark recesses of the house. Despite Emily's protestations, Peter circled the property occasionally calling out with an interesting tidbit.

"Well, I'll be. There's another wing back here. Honestly, this house is like a maze! Just how large is this property, anyway?" He got no response from her. "Emily, stop being such a scaredy cat. There's an amazing view back this way and you're missing it all!" As he made his way back to the front yard, the limo came into view.

Emily straightened up to give herself a last once-over in the mirror. "Peter, that must be them! It's about time."

The limo pulled up beside the sports car and Emily breathed a sigh of relief as she made out the shadowy figure of Schlocker through the tinted backseat window. She appreciated always knowing where she stood with someone, and Schlocker was a man who always made his stance, and his opinion of you, abundantly clear. His no-nonsense demeanor matched hers to a 't.'

Schlocker grabbed onto the door handle, wrenching it this way and that, oblivious to Anne, who was pointing up at the front to indicate the driver would have to let them out. Schlocker fumbled and fumed until Bruno opened the door and he nearly tumbled out onto the ground. Bruno offered him a hand, which he swatted away. Gathering his dignity from the dust, Schlocker approached Emily, transforming instantly from grouch to gracious. "Ah, my dear Ms. Howe. So good to see you here. And the young Mr. Howe?"

Peter held out a hand in greeting, "Hello there, Shocker."

"*Schlocker.*" He took Peter's hand without dropping his cigar and held it in a vise. Peter merely smiled back, musing over the obsession that men, such as this lawyer, always seemed to have with turning a simple handshake into a show of their brute strength. *Napoleon Complex*, he thought.

"Good to see you, my boy! Petey, this is my secretary, Miss Morse." Schlocker's forceful pumping an uncomfortable number of times left wet shreds of tobacco in Peter's palm. Peter smiled through gritted teeth at Anne, who had finally caught up with them.

She offered Peter a shy smile and extended her hand. Peter put his out then, remembering the tobacco, wiped his hand on his trousers before offering it to her once more with a "How do you do?"

"Good, thank you!" The two locked eyes momentarily, something passing between them — a something that was interrupted by Bruno's abrupt approach.

"And I'm Bruno, sir."

"Well," Peter said. "How are you, Bruno?"

Bruno hadn't been expecting Peter to offer his hand, having served as a chauffeur or other manner of servant for so many years. Uncertain how to proceed, he switched his cap from one hand to the other. Flustered, he removed his glove to shake hands with Peter, wishing that the world would do away with such pleasantries entirely.

He turned to face Emily, his hand still extended. "And this is Mrs. Howe, then?" Emily pointedly ignored his attempt to greet her, crossing her arms. She eyed him contemptuously.

"Oh, no no, Bruno! It's Miss Howe. That's my sister, Emily."

"Oh, I do beg your pardon."

Schlocker, who had suddenly remembered that Anne existed, motioned toward her by way of introduction. "Emily, this is my —"

Emily cut him off with a wave of her hand. "Let's just skip the rest of this, Schlocker, and get to business. I want to get a look at this place. It certainly is… large, isn't it?"

Peter chimed in. "I'll say. I was checking out the property and it just seems to go on forever! I wonder how much acreage you have here. What is it, Bruno? Maybe two acres or so?"

Emily shot Peter a look and he shut his mouth. She resumed her authority. "As I was saying, we should get to business, shouldn't we?"

Bruno shuffled toward the front of the group to lead them toward the house. "Yes, yes. I'm quite overdue and the children will be waiting. If you follow me up the drive I'll show you where you can park your machine. And if I may make a request… I hope you will be tactful with the children. They are not used to strangers, and they can become rather — um — wild, if encouraged."

Bruno was met by a contingent of blank stares. In the space of the silence, he motioned them up the front steps.

Chapter Eleven

From inside the house came sounds of childish excitement. Anxious footsteps and lilting laughter carried through the halls. The front door popped open, releasing Virginia and Elizabeth scrambling to take their places. They had clearly put a great deal of effort into their appearance, their hair neatly combed and secured with comically oversized velvet bows. They crossed their hands and stood, poised, the very model of good behavior. In the dirty glass of the door behind them, Ralph's excited face peeked out.

Schlocker led the group with a briefcase in hand. He stopped at the top step to marvel at the two girls. "Well! Look how adorable! The young misses Merrye! Don't they look like perfect little dolls! Now let me guess. You must be Elizabeth!" he declared to Virginia, who did not correct him but smiled and curtsied.

The mischievous look in her eye worried Bruno, who'd seen it many times before. He corrected Schlocker. "No, no. Virginia. This is Elizabeth." Bruno pointed to the other girl, who took her turn to curtsy. She dipped her head but her eyes stayed trained on Schlocker in a cold stare of contempt.

Emily, Peter, and Anne followed Schlocker and Bruno up.

Schlocker turned to Bruno. "Elizabeth and Virginia." He pointed to each of the girls in turn. "Yes, indeed. And the young master Merrye? Is he about?"

"Ralph, I believe, is within."

Virginia, excited at the mention of Ralph, sang his name quietly. "Ralphie, Ralphie, Ralphie."

A look of warmth, a sort of understanding, passed over Peter's face as he took in the sight of the two, if he was honest, rather pitiful girls. "Look, Emily. They're perfect little ladies, aren't they?"

"Yes," Elizabeth repeated. "Perfect little ladies."

Virginia crouched at dirty pane to surprise Ralph who was still peering at them from beneath the edge of a dirty shade, blinking. Virginia moved in closer to press her face against the pane. The siblings giggled, smashing their faces into the glass from opposite sides and imitating each other. "Ralphie, Ralphie, Ralphie!" Virginia cried.

Emily roiled with disgust. "There it is again! That animal. Peter, that's the thing that jumped out at me before. I told you!" She pointed an accusing finger at Ralph's giggling figure.

Even Schlocker was puzzled by her reaction. "Why, Emily. That's just... well, what is...?" he puzzled.

"Oh," Peter answered. "While we were waiting for you, Emily walked up to the house. I guess she ran into... him?"

Virginia pulled back from the window to face Emily, leaving Ralph framed in the glass of the door like a sort of freakshow poster, motionless and smiling. Virginia's eyes bored into Emily, angry at her animosity toward Ralph. She did not like this lady. *Not one bit.*

Bruno's face flushed red with embarrassment. For the children. For himself. But when he caught Virginia's eye, he registered her look and the mortification gave way to the cold sweat of fear. Bruno coughed into his hand, an attempt to hide what he felt.

Peter stepped up to the door and squatted down to face Ralph, eye-to-eye. "Big for his age, isn't he?" he inquired.

He waggled his fingers at Ralph, who, realizing that he had been noticed, panicked. Jerking his thumb from his mouth, he disappeared back into the gloom of the rooms. Taken aback, Peter locked eyes with Virginia and laughed. "He likes to play, doesn't he, Virginia?"

Virginia nodded, excited by the attention.

Bruno corralled everyone at the entrance. There was no use in further delaying the inevitable. "Please, do come inside. *Virginia!*"

Virginia's giggles ceased on command and Peter broke away. Wondering if he'd gotten her into trouble, Peter winked at her by way of apology. Virginia curtsied to Bruno in reply and resumed her former ladylike structure. "Yes, Bruno!"

Chapter Twelve

Schlocker could no longer contain his curiosity. He pushed his way to the front of the group and entered the home with Emily a short step behind. They stepped into the foyer, eyes alight with dollar signs as they scanned the home's fine furnishings which, while decidedly dusty, appeared to their novice eyes to be mostly of antique — and expensive — origin.

Like little dolls, straight and proper, Virginia and Elizabeth stood at attention against the wall, rigid perma-smiles plastered across their faces. Peter and Anne huddled close together at the rear of the group. If anyone else had been paying attention, it would have been clear that they were hitting it off.

Schlocker, emboldened upon his entry into the house, takes on a new attitude of familiarity. "Now ladies, this is your auntie Emily."

The girls' smiles were icy. Through gritted teeth, Virginia whispered to her sister. "I don't like that lady."

"And this," Schlocker said, "is your uncle, Peter."

The girls gave Peter a wave. "Elizabeth and Virginia. Those certainly are pretty names for two pretty young ladies. And this is Miss…"

Anne stepped forward. "Anne. My name is Anne. It's very nice to meet you." Her way was warm and unbothered.

Virginia curtsied again. Under Bruno's direction she had practiced and perfected her curtsy as a matter of the weekly "social skills" lessons that he had insisted upon. She wasn't about to waste all that practice now.

Elizabeth didn't move but she could not resist flashing a grin at her uncle Peter. Virginia, sensing Elizabeth's interest in him, shoved herself in front of her sister and threw out one more curtsy, just for good measure.

Peter backed away, a bit embarrassed, to wander into the adjoining drawing room. "And where is… ah… Ralph?"

The mere mention of Ralph's name set Virginia to jumping with excitement. Her composure completely stripped away, she pushed past Peter into the drawing room, where she spun herself in tight circles, again screaming, "Ralphie! Ralphie! Ralphie!"

"*Ungggghhh,*" came the reply.

Virginia followed the sound of Ralphie's moaning greeting to the square dumbwaiter opening and leaned into the shaft to call his name again. "*Ralphieeee*?"

The rest of the group had joined her by now, watching with confusion as she shouted into the darkness. Bruno called from the other side of the room. "Virginia! You stop playing and get your brother up here. No more teasing!"

As if performing, Virginia faced the others and slowly turned the dumbwaiter's crank handle. It creaked and groaned, struggling against the weight of a human inside. Slowly, the figure of Ralph, squatting in a fetal position with his thumb in his mouth, arose from below. Virginia reached out to pat his shiny head and Ralph responded by resting a hand on Virginia's cheek.

While Emily reeled back in disgust, Peter stepped forward to approach Ralph. Unsure of whether to offer a hand in greeting, he settled for patting the boy on the shoulder. "Hey, he's just a big kid, Emily. He's all right. Aren't you, Ralph?"

Ralph's head waggled back and forth, up and down, perhaps in response to Peter's query, perhaps not.

Bruno was relieved at Peter's reaction to the boy. "Yes, it's as you say, sir. A big kid. Exactly!"

While Peter engaged in a good-natured game of peek-a-boo with Ralph, Schlocker edged closer to get a look, thrusting his hand right in the boy's face. Leaning down as if to examine him, he went so far as to slip a finger into the side of Ralph's mouth and pull back his cheek. Ralph, unsure of how to react, turned his fearful gaze to Peter.

"Oh, come now. Schlocker. I don't think any of that is necessary, now, is it?"

"Hmm," Schlocker replied as he unhanded Ralph to offer his professional diagnosis.

"*Non compos mentis.* The whole lot of them! *Non compos menti.* I might have suspected as much. I'd say we have arrived not a moment too soon."

"*Non compos menti?*" Peter said.

"Yes! It would seem so. Why, I wouldn't be surprised if there were criminal charges involved here! These children should be in the care of the state!"

Emily stared down Bruno, a crude attempt at intimidation. To his credit, Bruno merely raised his chin, ignoring the obvious barbs.

Schlocker snapped his fingers at Anne, who scrambled to produce her steno pad to take down his speech. "Now, look here, Bruno. May I say I don't think you quite realize just how very serious all of this is."

Emily nodded in smug agreement. While the group tossed looks of concern at each other and Schlocker droned on to Anne, Bruno's eyes caught a movement in the corner of the room.

Elizabeth stalked the perimeter, carrying knick-knacks back

and forth and absently dusting as she made her way to join Virginia and Ralph. Peter continued to make faces at Ralph who, clearly enjoying the attention, had not given up his spot in the dumbwaiter.

"Look at them, Bruno," said Schlocker. "These children are obviously in need of qualified professional care. Wouldn't you agree?"

"I'm sure there is a great deal to be said for that, sir. But I made a solemn promise to the late master. Their dear father, god rest his soul... I promised that I would never allow their unfortunate malady to become the object of public scrutiny."

"Nonsense! The days when we hid our insane away behind walls of shame went out with that — that old car of yours!" Shlocker elbowed Emily in her side, cuing her to chuckle along with him.

"Insane? Oh no, sir. Again, I believe that you misunderstand. The children's condition is unlike anything you have seen before."

Virginia and Elizabeth stood stock still, hands behind their backs in their "perfect little ladies" pose, staring the adults down.

"They're talking about us, Virginia."

"I know, Elizabeth."

Peter sidled up to Bruno, speaking under his breath. "Bruno, ah, just what sort of malady is this, you mentioned? I mean, I've been around kids with... uh, conditions before, but this seems..."

"Well, sir. It is a very rare condition. As I understand it, it's a regression to a sort of, not to be crude, but a state of deterioration. Deterioration of not just mental faculties but the things that make us feel normal human emotions. A rotting away of the brain, of the part of our humanity, so to speak. It begins in late childhood and continues to progress steadily, rather like... *paresis* in its later stages."

Peter's jaw dropped open. "Oh. Really? That bad? Is it...?"

"Fatal? It's all right to ask, sir. I find it is best to be honest in such matters. Of course, the children only know as much as they can understand. But yes, tragically it will shorten their lifespan."

"I'm sorry to hear it," Peter said. "I had no idea that their condition was this serious. Such a strange sounding disease."

"Indeed," Bruno replied. "The Merrye family, or this branch anyway, has been afflicted for generations with outcroppings among its members. I'm very much afraid that this generation will be the last."

Both men regarded the children with pity: the girls standing straight and pretty and Ralph, who had hopped from his perch and skipped in off-kilter circles.

"You don't say so, Bruno."

"And if I may, sir, I am sad to say that I consider it a blessing. To continue this line would be... Well, it would only result in so much more unnecessary suffering"

"What a terrible shame. You're so very kind to be taking care of these children."

Having wrapped up his speech, Schlocker circled the room with Emily, each excitedly pointing at the various vases, statues and other potential valuables that lined the oiled oak shelves.

Emily's eyes caught Bruno's. She held his gaze even as Schlocker prattled on about the value of a flower patterned Lenox gravy boat. "Schlocker, don't you think we should be getting on with the business at hand? I don't want to be here any longer than necessary." She pointedly tore her gaze from Bruno so that she could sweep the room with a dramatic look of disgust.

"Yes, of course. Forgive me. Right this way, please." Bruno steered the group through an archway and toward a grand wooden dining table. Brittle with disuse, the chairs groaned as the party pulled them out to sit.

Virginia skipped over to station herself over Peter's shoulder. Elizabeth joined her, the two quietly elbowing each other in hopes of edging in closer to him. Bruno loudly cleared his throat and the girls fell still, one to each side of Peter.

Schlocker twirled the lock on his leather briefcase and, with great ceremony, withdrew a folder, a leather folio, and a sheaf of papers, which he spread across the table. Emily picked up a form, squinting at it in the dim light. She huffed loudly and hopped up to raise the window blind, exposing glass that was nearly opaque with dust.

Schlocker thumbed through a stack of papers and stopped suddenly. "Ah, Nedrick."

"Hmm. What's that, sir?" Bruno asked.

"One other question, Bruno. I should like to know the whereabouts of certain other members of the Merrye family – the two sisters of Titus W. Merrye, and a brother named, I believe, Nedrick Merrye, if alive."

Bruno reeled back as if punched by the unexpected query. When he had gathered his wits, he said, "Alive? Well, one might say that, sir. But…"

Virginia and Elizabeth, still in their respective stations, leaned back behind their uncle to whisper to each other. "They're talking about Uncle Ned!" Virginia said.

"I know," Elizabeth replied.

Emily had had it with the circuitous conversation. "This is ridiculous. Come on now, Bruno. Don't beat around the bush. Are they around or not?"

Bruno hemmed and hawed, shifting nervously from foot to foot, suddenly very aware that his every word was being taken down by Anne. The entire table faced him in silence. Bruno was not inclined to lie. He was, if anything, occasionally honest to a fault. And so he racked his brain for a reply honest enough that could reveal little of their real situation. But as he never was good under pressure, he blurted out the first thing that came to mind, a statement that was neither honest nor helpful to his cause.

"Well, that's a good question. You know… I can't recall

when…" Bruno stopped to clear his throat. "You see, I really haven't kept track of the older members of the family in recent years, Miss Howe. You see, their condition advanced to the point that it became necessary to put them in a… uh, a private institution of some sort."

Emily clutched at her pearls — yes, *her pearls* — in mock mortification. "You mean to say that you have left your own family members alone in an institution, without so much as corresponding with them?"

Bruno's mouth opened and closed, futilely searching for the words that would make this situation better. The only thing that escaped his paralyzed mouth was a low groan.

Peter turned to his sister. "Emily, come on now. Let's give old Bruno here a break. Why, look at all that he has to deal with already, taking care of three — let's face it — very sick children. And now us coming here must be a real shock." Beneath the table, Emily kicked Peter
in the shin.

Bruno nodded blankly, muttering, "Yes. It is a bit of a shock. A shock. Yes."

Schlocker extended his arms wide, a theatrical gesture that nearly knocked the pen from his beleaguered secretary's hand. "Yes, Bruno. You certainly do have your hands full. My good man! Am I to understand that you — the family chauffeur — have been solely responsible for the care of this entire estate and these three minor children?"

Bruno nodded. "I never thought of it quite like that, sir. You see, I promised the master…as I said… that I would take care of them."

Emily replied. "Yes, yes. We know all about that. Listen, Schlocker. It's been a long trip and I'd like to get freshened up and off my feet for a while. I see no reason that we can't go through this after dinner."

Bruno looked puzzled. "Dinner?"

Schlocker gathered the sheaves and piles of paper which he

shoveled back into his suitcase. "Yes, yes. It is about dinner time, now isn't it, Bruno? Oh, and as a matter of fact, we intend to stay the night here."

Bruno could not hide the horror he felt. His eyes went wide, a sheen of sweat gathered above his brow. Bruno had to touch his shirt and will himself to calm his racing heart. "Oh no," he said. "We would love to have you, but I'm afraid that's quite impossible. Merrye House is not prepared to accommodate guests."

Emily acted shocked again and she played the part with the flair of a *Sunset Boulevard* auditionee, her mouth and eyes both rounding with utter contempt. "There may be a difference of opinion as to who is the guest and who is the host here. You do have food in the house, don't you?" She cast glances at each of the three children in turn. "What do you and the children eat?"

"Our diet is quite austere, Miss Howe, as I mentioned earlier. But I suppose we might find... something."

Elizabeth, Ralph, and Virginia stood by obediently. But if one were to examine them more closely, one might catch the glimpse of a sly smile parting the corners of Elizabeth's lips.

Chapter Thirteen

Merrye House stood tall and lonely in the late afternoon sun. The shadows had begun their nightly creep across the house, the skeletons of the trees growing taller with each passing moment. At the corner of the property, far from the porch, a figure skittered about the dry scrub, its movements the irregular gait of a many-legged insect. Could it have been… a spider?

An arm darted out from behind a dying bit of bush, followed by the rest of Virginia's body. She stayed close to the ground amongst the weeds and fungi, her arms and legs splayed out about her, spider-like, her torso parallel to the ground. Pausing to investigate the base of each bush and tree, locomoting about the yard in that strangely uncanny side to side way. She froze, cocked her head to listen. Virginia squinted at the ground, whispering between her barely-parted teeth.

"I smell a bug!" By this time she had come upon an impressive hunk of granite, a piece near the size of her head. She pulled her belly up off the ground and pulled the rock up over her head, lacing both hands around it, poised to attack.

"I see a bug. A big black juicy bug!" The rock landed with a satisfying thud. Virginia giggled, which gave way to a high-pitched squeal of delight.

Ralph, who was engaged in a hunt of his own nearby, let out a shriek of commiseration.

A cat prowled lazy and careless in the weedy shrubs. She picked her way through the fungi, blissfully unaware that a predator lay in wait for her. Suddenly, a hunched figure leapt forward to pounce on the luckless creature.

Virginia watched as Ralph pinned the pitiful creature to the ground.

* * *

The kitchen door swung open to usher in Bruno, having donned a stark white chef hat. He deposited a steaming silver serving platter on the table and stopped to watch Virginia lay out place settings, pride plain on his face.

"I'm proud of you, Virginia. You're doing so well," Bruno said.

As Virginia straightened the silverware setting before her and smiled up at Bruno, Elizabeth skipped into the room. "Ralph is ready, Bruno."

"Thank you, Elizabeth. Virginia, you may bring Ralph down now."

"Ralphie, Ralphie, Ralphie!" Virginia dropped the silverware and darted from the room, her job forsaken.

Bruno sighed and picked up the forgotten silverware from the floor. He swiped the cutlery across his pants and, deeming them adequately polished — *there's a five second rule after all* — laid them out beside a chipped blue china plate.

"Ralphie! Ralphie!" Virginia cried as she skipped over to the drawing room dumbwaiter. She called down into the dark shaft and cranked the handle in gleeful anticipation.

Bruno's low voice echoed from the dining room. "Dinner is served!"

Emily jumped from her seat beside Schlocker. She straightened her dress, making a great show of wiping her skirt clean of any invisible dust. "It's about time! I might have just rotted away to skin and bones sitting here."

Peter offered a hand to Anne who, seated as she was in a terribly unstable bit of fluff and velvet that passed for a chair, accepted it with a quiet nod of thanks.

Emily shot Anne a look and huffed. "Hmm. Wouldn't it be nice if Peter could show his own sister that same sort of respect?"

Peter ignored the rebuff and allowed his sister to take the lead. Peter rubbed his stomach and turned to Anne, "Boy, I could use a meal! I can't wait to see what's on the menu."

"Oh yes," Anne said. She lowered her voice, a polite whisper. "I was about to get desperate enough to go sneak a piece of fruit from that orange tree out back!"

Peter and Anne chuckled, once more drawing his sister's attention. As they passed by Virginia, the dumbwaiter creaked to a halt, releasing Ralph from its square confines.

He dropped down from the conveyance, revealing his fresh outfit: a '20s style short pant suit of dark blue crushed velvet. The Little Lord Fauntleroy getup had clearly seen better days and was several sizes too tight; the seams buckled and stretched under the pressure of Ralph's movements. He patted the ruffles at his neckline, showing off his outfit.

"Hi, Ralph," said Peter. "Oh wow. Would you look at that, Emily? I do believe we are underdressed for the event."

Ralph smiled widely showing a mishmashed dental catastrophe of missing teeth and too-sharp canines and patted the ruffles once more to Peter's delight. Emily shuddered. Virginia took Ralph's hand to lead him to the table.

Emily's voice dripped with disdain. "Oh yes, Peter. Isn't that adorable?"

As if on cue, Virginia popped up behind Peter and pulled a chair out for him, pointing forcefully at the table. "Oh," Peter said and took his seat. "Thank you, Virginia."

Emily waited in vain for the same but when no one took her

to her seat, she snatched a chair out from under the table and plopped down. Schlocker claimed his spot at the head of the table and was greedily eyeing the large silver platter in the center.

Although the table had already been set, Bruno handed Ralph a few more napkins to give out. He circled the table, giggling, a whirling dervish stopping only to toss wrinkled napkins in the general direction of the guests.

Emily threw her hands up in front of her face each time he passed her field of vision, while Peter and Anne clapped their hands in delighted approval of the pleasure that Ralph took in his work.

"Come now, come on, Ralph," Bruno said and held his arms out to encourage the man-boy toward him. "You've done a fine job but it's time to eat now."

Ralph paid him no mind, instead forcing himself in the little space between Emily and Peter's chairs that he might better examine Anne's face. He twisted his neck to observe her features — the pink painted upturned lips, her pert little nose. Anne smiled politely, humoring his innocent curiosity.

Schlocker shook his head. "Emily, my dear!" he proclaimed. "There is absolutely no doubt left in my mind. What we have here is a most clear cut prima facie open and shut case!"

Elizabeth and Virginia paraded back and forth, taking turns at laying out covered platters of food while Bruno corralled Ralph toward his seat — a taller version of the others, it looked rather like a Victorian high chair built for a teenager.

Bruno tucked the boy into the chair with some effort — he was getting old after all and Ralph was the size of a high school freshman — and buckled him in with worn leather straps.

Schlocker watched the events unfold, his disbelief growing by the minute. *How could they have gotten so lucky,* he wondered. "Yes, open and shut!"

Bruno turned from Ralph, alarmed. "A case? Why, sir, I'm not sure what you mean..."

Emily waved him away, turning back to Schlocker. "Great! Now, what I want to know is just what is it all worth in dollars and cents?"

With Peter and Anne engaged in their own quiet conversation and the girls now seated quietly at the table watching them, Bruno took his own place. He shook out his napkin dramatically, holding it up for all to see. The children dutifully followed suit, shaking out their wrinkled napkins and placing them in their laps. "Good job, children," he said, though there was no one to hear him.

Schlocker and Emily were nose to nose in greedy excitement. "Hmm," Schlocker frowned, thinking. "That's difficult to say from this juncture. Perhaps, after an audit. Ah, Miss Morse, let me have Schedule B."

When Anne, who was still deep in her conversation with Peter did not respond, Schlocker — who was accustomed to Anne's immediate response — cleared his throat loudly and called out again. "MISS MORSE!"

"Hmm?" Anne's laugh died off and she turned, at attention, to her boss.

"I said, let me have a schedule B, Miss Morse. If you aren't too busy."

Anne looked at the table and then at her empty hands. "Oh, well, I didn't bring the paperwork to the dinner table. I thought —"

"You thought," Schlocker proclaimed. "I do not pay you to think, Miss Morse. Now if you'll go and get those papers..."

Anne excused herself to retrieve Schlocker's briefcase. Ralph scanned the table, his eyes settling on Emily's drumming fingers. He watched with intense interest for a moment, balled up his fist and pounded it on his tray. The irregular rhythm excited Virginia who joined in the game, banging her own fists on the table in imitation of Ralph. Elizabeth took the cue and armed herself with a fork and knife, which she clanged together. The children's laughter and the raucous music rose in volume, leaving poor Bruno to helplessly call out over the cacophony.

"Now, children! Children! Please!"

Emily watched Bruno in quiet disgust at this quiet, kind man and his gentle ways. "Schlocker," she said. "You must put a stop to this."

When Schlocker's ineffectual calls of "now see here" failed to quiet the din, Emily jumped from her chair to scream, "Now that is enough! This is utter nonsense and I will not be quiet while these children are allowed to behave like... well..."

The children had quieted, the silverware returned to the table, their hands still. All eyes were on her. "You are allowing them to behave like animals!" she concluded.

Peter sucked in his breath, shocked at his sister's outburst. "Emily, I don't think that was necessary. They're just children after all."

Bruno's eyes misted over, his chin tucking deep into his chest. "No, no, Peter. She is right. The children's behavior is unacceptable. I —"

Anne had reappeared and, alarmed at the state of the table, frozen in place, Schlocker's briefcase dangling off her arm.

"Well, come on then, Ms. Morse!" Schlocker commanded. "And I must say that, if anything, this little show has only deepened my concern for the welfare of these minor children."

Virginia whispered through her gritted teeth. "Elizabeth, they are talking about us again..."

Elizabeth pinched her sister's arm to shush her. "Yes, and I want to hear what they are saying."

Virginia frowned and then, her lip quivered with a sudden realization... "They are trying to take us from Bruno, aren't they?"

Elizabeth responded with another pinch and a loud *shhhhhhh*.

Schlocker was, at least for the moment, winding down. He

pointed an impatient finger at Anne and yelled, "The Schedule B, Miss Morse!"

His sour tone was enough to both rouse Anne from her frozen state of anxiety and, conversely, send Ralph into a new fit of table-pounding.

Elizabeth took up her brother's rhythm with her spoon and fork — *clang, clang, clang!* Bruno arose from the table and leaned over, but before he could open his mouth to command quiet, Emily jumped up.

She splayed her hands across the table and scanned the faces that surrounded it. Her voice was calm but cutting, like shards of ice. "All of you, be quiet! I will have no more of this circus. Now, put your hands down in your lap and shut up so that we can eat like civilized human beings!"

"Oh," Bruno replied. "I'm afraid we are still waiting on the main dish. It's still in the oven, but… it shouldn't be long now."

"Oh, of course. We'll sit here all night waiting, I suppose."

Elizabeth dropped her spoon, but she held the fork out in front of her, the tines aimed in the direction of Emily's looming figure. Ralph quieted himself by sticking his thumb deep into his mouth.

Bruno sat back down, torn between the relief of the quiet and the utter humiliation of Emily's command over his charges.

Her mission accomplished, Emily took her seat once more. Elizabeth's cold stare never left the woman's face.

Peter cleared his throat. "Well, then, uh… how much longer do you think dinner will be, Mr.… I mean, Bruno?"

"The timer should be going off any minute now," Bruno answered. "I'm sorry for the delay, but as I mentioned earlier, we don't often have the… pleasure… of guests, so we had to do a bit of, uh, creative catering, if you will. I do believe you will enjoy what Virginia and Ralph have cooked up for us."

"I'm certain we will," Peter replied.

"Yes," Anne added "It smells wonderful."

Even as she said it, her mouth turned slightly downward

with worry, for the scent emanating from the kitchen was...
unusual, to say the least. The familiar smell of meat mingled
with a sickly-sweet odor that reminded Anne of nothing so
much as the time she had discovered a one week old dead
mouse beneath the kitchen sink. A wave of shame washed over
her when her eyes met Bruno's kind face and she pushed the
nasty thought to the back of her mind.

Emily watched over Schlocker's shoulder as he perused the
text, his finger tracing the outline of the letter, lips moving
silently in time. "Miss Morse! Schedule C as well." Schlocker
thrusts a hand toward her, wiggling his fingers impatiently.

"Of course. Yes," Anne replied, thumbing through the pile of
documents before handing him a similarly dense document
with an oversized letter C at the top. "Right here, Mr.
Schlocker."

Ding! When the metallic chime issued from the kitchen
Virginia hopped up from her seat. Clapping her hands, she
skipped off to the kitchen. Peter comically licked his chops for
Ralph's entertainment and the boy happily returned the
gesture.

For Schlocker's part, he was still head-deep in paperwork,
perusing the endless columns of text and mumbling while Anne
attempted to point out — to no avail — the object of his search.
She pointed at a column. "Right there, Mr. Schlocker."

Shlocker dismissed Anne with a wave and turned the papers
toward Emily. "Aha!" he proclaimed. "Of course, this estimate
represents only the visible part of the iceberg so to speak. On
the basis of the other information that we gather, we may be
able to project the total."

Peter interjected with a loud *ahem!* and jerked his head
toward the kitchen doorway where Virginia stood in a low
curtsy, oversized platter balanced precariously on one hand.

Bruno watched her as a fond parent takes in a child's recital.
"Ladies and gentlemen, dinner is served!" he said.

Shlocker craned his head away from the document at last,

shoving the papers at Anne, who struggled to put them in some kind of order before stacking them back in the briefcase. Schlocker rubbed his hands together in anticipation. "Well! At last!"

Virginia sat the platter at the edge of the table and slid it toward the center before taking her seat.

"Thank you, Virginia." Peter said. "Hungry, Miss Morse?"

"Oh yes! It smells… delicious."

Bruno crossed the table to pat Virginia on the shoulder. "That was real good, Virginia. Thank you."

Virginia crooked a finger at Bruno, who bowed down to hear her soto voice. "Can I feed Winifred now? I know she's hungry."

Bruno reeled back from her. He shook it off and took Virginia's hand. "No. Not now. Winifred will have to wait just a little bit. She can now, can't she?" Virginia would not be assuaged; she shook her head doubtfully.

"Bruno, you know if she gets hungry, she'll start to look for something to eat."

The thought of Winifred running free sent a cold chill of terror up Bruno's spine. He thought fast — *get it over with* — and changed tacts. "Very well, then. I guess you'd better feed her. But hurry up before dinner gets cold."

"Oh, I will! I will!" she said, as she skipped from the room.

Bruno took his seat once more and spread his hands across the table. "Well, here we are. It certainly is lovely to have guests here in the Merrye House. We're not accustomed to it, not these days. It's been a long, long time since we have had the pleasure of dinner with guests. This is a rather rare treat, I must say."

Bruno stalled, hemming and hawing, one eye on the doorway. When he saw Virginia streak by with a glass jar in hand, his heart skipped a beat. She caught Bruno's gaze and winked at him before skittering away.

* * *

Virginia carefully rolled down the top of the drawing room desk, peering into the rows of pigeonholes and letter slots. She crouched down, eye level with the oiled wooden drawers and whispered, "Winifred?"

She stared down the dark recesses of the desk's furthest corners, waiting for a response. When none was forthcoming, she dropped a hand to retrieve the jar at her feet. She lifted it up to her face, squinting but the greasy film that coated the jar obscured its contents.

Virginia unscrewed the lid and tilted the jar onto its side to release a plump brown cockroach. Virginia crouched down once more. She heard a sound, a familiar tippy-tap, followed by feather light scratching and then — in a flash — a palm-sized creature, a tangle of pinkish-brown prickly limbs that rushed forward helter-skelter to tear into the hapless cockroach.

"Winifred!" Virginia exclaimed.

As the last of the cockroach disappeared into Winifred's mouth, a companion emerged from another of the desk's far pigeonholes. This tarantula, larger and darker in color, approached and seeing the last of the potential meal slipping away, lashed out at Winifred. Virginia wagged her finger at the creature.

"Barney! You be nice! And Winifred! Shame on you. Why didn't you tell me that Barney came back?"

"Virginia! We're waiting for you," Bruno called.

Virginia sighed heavily. "Oh, of course." She blew the spiders a kiss. "I'll come and see you later," she said, as she closed the insects' enclosure.

The guests' heads turned in relieved greeting as Virginia entered the room.

"Well, finally!" Emily proclaimed.

Bruno stood behind Ralph, tying the strings of a stained yellow kerchief-come-bib around his neck while Ralph smiled widely at the guests.

"Take your seat, Virginia," Bruno said.

Virginia curtsied and took her seat beside her sister, who promptly poked her in the ribs. "Where were you?" Elizabeth whispered. To her visible disappointment, Virginia did not reply.

Bruno returned to the head of the table where he stood in place, the largest silver platter stationed before him. When he was certain that all eyes were on him, he dropped his hand to lift the trancher's cover with a theatrical flourish. "Voila! Dinner is served!"

While Virginia let out a loud "Ooooh!" and Ralph clapped his hands in earnest anticipation, the other guests went coldly silent.

Emily's mouth dropped open, disgust written across her features. Schlocker's cigar slipped from his lips; this might have been the first time in decades that he could not find his words. Peter and Anne glanced first at the platter and then at each other, gauging whether the other was as shocked as them.

The four legged animal on the silver trancher was roasted, dressed, and garnished to perfection, its crispy skin glistening with fat. The guests' scrunched their faces in confusion.

Emily threw her napkin down. "Fine. If no one else is going to say anything, I will. What is that?"

"That" was a smallish mammal about the size of a housecat. Bruno opened his mouth to speak, but Peter jumped in before he could get anything out. "Why, it's rabbit obviously, Emily. Not bad, Bruno. Looks done to a turn."

"Why, thank you, sir. I hope you enjoy it. We're most fortunate to have meat for our guests this evening. You see, we're vegetarians."

Schlocker screwed his face up, a mixture of disgust and incredulity. "Vegetarians? Well, I suppose I should not be surprised. In addition to the other, uh, irregularities..." Schlocker turned to Emily in a fever. "Why, these children haven't even had proper nutrition.

Elizabeth wrinkled her nose. "It's dead. We do not eat dead things."

Schlocker shook his head at Bruno. "Good lord, man. Why on earth?"

Bruno muttered, "The master asked me…"

Emily interrupted Bruno with a wave of her hand. "Don't say it. We know. You made a promise to take care of the children. You've told us several times!"

Bruno's reply is righteous and firm. "It was no whim, I assure you madame. The master understood only too well the danger —"

Peter interjected. "What danger?"

Emily eyed her brother then Bruno. "Yes, what danger, Bruno?"

Bruno stuttered, a repeating "I-I-I…" before stopping to regain his poise. "That is to say," he continued, "The master believed, and I think that you should know, that tasting flesh — meat — might quicken the progress of their condition. You understand, and therefore…"

Emily threw her hands to the skies as if in heavenly praise. "You can throw away your hearing aids, folks!" She exclaimed. "Because now we have heard it all! That is patently ridiculous."

Bruno's face went slack.

Peter shot Emily a piercing look. "Emily, really? I don't know that this level of dramatics is necessary. I find this all very interesting. Now wait a minute, Bruno. Are you saying like that old story about lion cubs being tame till they have their first taste of fresh meat?"

"I'm afraid it's more serious than that, Mr. Howe," Bruno replied.

"Huh. Fascinating."

Her voice hoarse from her endless haranguing, Emily turned to Peter. "Whatever it is — rabbit or — oh, whatever, I pass."

Peter answered her with studied nonchalance. "More for us then, huh, everyone? Looks pretty good to me. I'll carve!"

Bruno's face lit up. "Very good sir. Please, carry on."

Bruno passed the platter from his side of the table to Elizabeth, who passed to Virginia. She held it close to her, teasing Peter with its presence. She turned to him and pushed it out, away from her but when his hands reached the handle she pulled it back out of his reach, a silly game. She balanced the platter on one flat palm and picked up the oversized carving knife with the other.

Although she did nothing more than hold it there, Bruno's panic was instant. Having finally settled down to eat, he found himself back on his feet, at the ready, just in case — oh, he dare not think it — *surely with guests here, she wouldn't...*

"Virginia, dear," Bruno said, fighting to keep a calm cadence in the face of the impending disaster. "Now, you pass that along to your Uncle Peter like a *good girl.*"

The tableau sat like that momentarily, Bruno's words hanging in the air and Peter, stock still, uncertain of how to react. Finally, Virginia smiled and passed the platter to her uncle, releasing them all to sigh with relief. She lowered her hand to offer Peter the knife, blade facing him. "Why, thank you Virginia," Peter said, as he deftly reached over the sharp tip to accept the handle.

Peter examined the trussed creature in front of him with its singed skin and trussed feet which, now that he had a chance to see them up close, looked like nothing so much as ... *cat paws?* Peter banished the horrific thought from his head, dismissing it as silly fancy. And, besides, all the guests were famished and it did smell, as Peter had said, *done to a turn.*

Peter prodded the roast, separating bone from sinew to dig into the juiciest parts of the carcass. He held a slice of meat out on a pronged fork toward Emily, who rebuked him with a wave of her hand.

"No, thank you, Peter, dear."

Just as Schlocker offered his plate to Peter, Bruno jumped in, as if he had forgotten to share something of great importance.

"Oh yes! And I would like you all to know that you have Ralph here to thank for providing it."

"Is that so?" Peter asked, "Well, good for you, Ralph!"

Schlocker, however, recoiled at the information, snatching his plate out of the path of the hunk of meat that hung from Peter's pronged serving fork. "I'll, uh, have something else."

Ralph's eyes glittered with pride, his fanged canines protruding through the wide smile. His lips stretched, grotesquely wide, to release a stream of drool that dripped down in tendrils. He pounded his silverware up and down on the table, chanting random syllables of clear delight.

Peter took up Anne's plate and slid a choice piece of haunch onto it. Although she eyed the food with more than a bit of suspicion, she did not object. "Thank you."

Schlocker's hands shot out, greedy. He reached for the closest covered vessel and raised the cover, peering at what appeared to him as a pile of juicy black sponge bits. He lifted some of the food with the serving spoon to better examine it.

"What do you call… this?" he asked. His stomach let out a gurgle, hunger and disgust fighting for his attention.

Bruno was elated at what he took as Schlocker's interest in the fare. "Ah, a rare treat for you, I'm sure. Our favorite dish. We call it, ah, souffled fungi."

Schlocker considered the spoonful for a moment, staring down into its dark, dripping contents. "What?" he asked again.

Emily let out a deep sigh. "Mushrooms, Schlocker. You know."

"Mushrooms? Oh, *fungi*. I see. I misheard him. Yes, mushrooms, of course" Schlocker grinned.

As his spoon dug into the vessel, Emily smiled at him. "I wouldn't worry about what kind of mushrooms…"

Schlocker gulped but piled a few spoonfuls on his plate.

Bruno continued on about the mushrooms. "Yes, One of our real staples, they grow quite freely about the grounds. They're quite good for you, I understand and this is our favorite way to prepare them."

Emily choked back a chuckle. Schlocker set his plate down, now eyeing his fungi stew with suspicion. "And did Ralph, uh…"

Bruno chuckled. "Oh, good heavens no, sir. Ralph doesn't know anything about mushrooms. Virginia provides these for us, and very well, too. You see, Virginia has an uncanny flair for selecting only non-poisonous mushrooms."

Schlocker, who was still staring down the pile of black slop, could feel pairs of eyes boring into him. He lifted his head, his gaze meeting Virginia's. Her expression was blank, a Mona Lisa with her straight lips and quiet, unmoving eyes.

Finally, Peter breaks the silence, reaching over Schlocker for the vessel of mushrooms.

"Come on, Schlocker. Let's not hog the good stuff."

When the lawyer didn't react, Peter snatched the silver serving spoon right out of his slack hand to serve a glob to Anne. Although uncertain, she smiled anyway and settled her plate in front of her.

Peter served liberal portions of the fungi to Elizabeth and Virginia. "Thank you, Uncle Peter," Elizabeth said.

"You are most welcome, Elizabeth," Peter replied.

With Peter's attention momentarily focused on Elizabeth, Virginia turned her body, shifting her body such that it blocked her sister entirely from her uncle's view. "Yes," she said. "Thank you so very much, Uncle Peter."

"And you are also welcome!"

Ralph's patience all but gone, he pounded his silverware again, demanding Peter's attention. He swung his plate back and forth, pushing it toward Emily. She refused to touch it, instead turning in the opposite direction and forcing Peter to rise from his seat.

He leaned across his sister — making no attempt to stay out of her space, as little brothers are wont to do — and accepted hooting Ralph's empty plate. Peter loaded it up with a heaping pile of fungi, which Ralph accepted with great excitement, flapping his hands above his head by way of thanks.

"Hey, Schlocker. Certainly can't say they're not polite now, can you?" Peter said.

Schlocker *harrumphed* in reply.

Bruno noted Emily's barren plate. "Miss Howe, I know that you've had a long trip. If you don't feel up to the heavier fare, perhaps you'd care for some fresh garden greens."

Bruno took up an oversized etched-glass salad bowl and passed it down the row. Each guest peeked into the bowl, but none stopped to serve themselves, Emily had already made up her mind about its contents.

Peter set down his knife to pass the bowl. "Yeah, try the salad, Emily. I know how you love greens." Peter clapped his hand to his mouth to hide the smirk in anticipation of his sister's reaction. He tore back into a hunk of meat, chewing with one eye on Emily.

For her part, she hadn't touched the bowl which, due to its position near the middle of the table at her place, revealed very little of its contents. She let out a derisive snort as she pulled the bowl towards herself. "Thank you, brother *dear*."

As it had been made clear that Peter would not serve her, Emily *ahemed* in the general direction of Schlocker who leapt to attention, scrape-scooting his chair to her side.

Bruno's jaw clenched. Oh, how he hated that awful sound of the metal chair leg buttons screeching across his fine wooden floor. *Such an affront to Merrye House!* But he held his tongue, watching as Schlocker fumbled with the tongs.

"Allow me," he cooed, as he dug into the bowl and lifted a clump of what appeared to be...

Emily let out a screech. "What *is* that?"

The mess of wiry greens were nothing more than undressed tumbleweed, that same brittle, dry grass that populated the dead land that Merrye House slept upon. Emily barely glanced at the "salad" before forcefully pushing Schlocker's hand away.

Ralph tossed his silverware — and all pretense of etiquette — to the floor. He inverted his plate, dumping the greasy shreds of meat directly onto his tray and buried his head in the gristly mess, licking and slurping the meat into his open maw.

Emily turned her body completely sideways, her back to Ralph and reached below the table to produce her fine alligator handbag. She fished out first a silver and turquoise pill box with a daisy clasp, and then a half-eaten bag of potato chips, which she dumped onto her plate. She lifted her purse, peering into it, searching and — "Aha!" dug out an untouched chocolate bar, which she added to the makeshift dinner assembling on her chipped china plate.

Schlocker's eyes darted from Emily's plate — a relative feast in said situation — to the dry greens dangling from the tongs in his hand, before serving himself a heaping helping of the dry mess.

Bruno watched the entire fiasco unfold from his spot at the head of the table.

Virginia and Elizabeth were doing a good job to be sure — picking politely at their plates, hiding their smirking smiles behind hands as they exchanged heated whispers. He was terribly proud of them, and even of Ralph who made up for his distinct lack of manners with his fangy smile of sheer exuberance.

But that Emily, he thought. His eyes dropped to the table, dark with a mix of mortification and disgust, the latter being a result of the former. *After all,* he reminded himself, *if anyone should be embarrassed, it's her. Such a lack of decorum. Why the children, even with their deficiencies, would never think to display such a lack of manners.*

Having reassured himself with such thoughts, he looked back up, taking comfort in the gristle-flecked smile of satisfaction being shared between Peter and Ralph.

Peter tucked in for another mouthful, pausing to chide Emily. "This is great. Emily, you don't know what you're missing!"

Bruno fairly beamed. "As I said, our diet is austere but most healthful, I can assure you."

Peter lifted his water glass, a toast to Bruno. "Well, my compliment to the chef." Ralph let out a food-filled screech of protest. "Chefs! Yes, of course. Here's to you, Ralph!" Peter caught the movement of a foreign object in his water. He dipped a pinkie nail into the glass to fish out the offending detritus and continued to drink.

"Oh, if only you had been here a few months ago," said Bruno. "We do have our favorite delicacies, but they're not in season right now."

Virginia, who had been angling for her Uncle Peter's attention for the whole of the meal, visibly brightened when Peter's gaze caught hers. She smiled widely as she dug an oversized serving spoon into a bowl of amorphous shapes covered in cream.

Unnerved by Virginia's unwavering stare, Peter cleared his throat and ventured conversation. "That certainly looks good, Virginia. What have you got there?"

Virginia raised her eyebrows and took another bite, the creamy sauce dripping from the corners of her lips. She put her fingertips on the bowl and scooted it in Peter's direction.

Before it could get to him, Bruno jumped up to intervene, pushing the container forcefully back to the girl's spot. "Oh no. You wouldn't want any of that, sir."

Virginia dug into the bowl again, making a dramatic show of enjoying the strange concoction.

Peter couldn't help his curiosity. What *was* that dish... he wondered, a thought that he regretted almost immediately. He stared, puzzling at the bowl's contents, letting out a little gasp at what he would have sworn was something *moving* beneath the layer of cream.

Emily smacked her brother's arm, tearing his attention away from Virginia's wriggling dinner long enough to shake off the movement as a trick of the mind. He chuckled to himself. *Yes, just my imagination.*

Emily leaned back in her chair, arms crossed tightly enough to compromise her circulation, and rounded on her brother. "Just how long does it take to eat, Peter?"

Peter licked his fingers, taking great delight in his sister's still-growing discomfort. "Oh, I am pretty hungry! I may just partake in seconds. That is, if Bruno doesn't mind."

Bruno nodded enthusiastically, passing the silver entree platter back his way via Virginia, who dropped the carcass to the side of Peter's place. The roast was nothing but stringy bits of crisp flesh clinging to spindly bones.

"We seem to have done a number on the rabbit!" Peter exclaimed. He wielded the carving knife, giving up all pretense of delicacy to dig and pick at the remains, flicking strings of meat to and fro.

Emily threw her hands to her mouth in disgust.

Peter scooped the pitiful pile of meat over onto his plate and turned to his sister. "What do you think about staying the night now, sister dear?"

Emily froze, unaccustomed as she was to being challenged, but quickly got her hackles back up. She uncrossed her arms and legs and scooted into the table, leaning forward into Peter's space to exclaim, "Oh, you couldn't drag me away from her!"

Schlocker, who had been quietly jawing at a mouthful of wiry greens, gulped down the fibrous goo to answer Emily. "Good show, my dear," he said through dry bites. "I'm with you. We will, of course, be staying the night so that we can better ascertain…"

Bruno raised his hands in dissent. "We love having guests but as I said, sir, that's just not possible. We —"

Schlocker was having none of it. "There's no more to say, Bruno. Look here. We —" he nodded toward Emily. "We want to be fair, you know. So, let's just make things as easy for all of us as we can, okay?"

Bruno shook his head sadly. *These people.* He had presided over the circus that was the arrival of these guests — *well, if one could call them that.* They had come unbidden and he had handled this most unseemly situation with decorum and the patience of a saint. But that patience was slipping away, if his stiff demeanor and stammering words were any indicator. "It's just that I — I —"

Emily cut in, dismissive. "This place is absolutely enormous! You cannot tell me there isn't room for a few guests. The sisters can move in together. And I'm sure, Bruno, that you and Ralph could share a room. It's just one night."

Peter noted Bruno's faltering good humor and attempted to cut in. "We could get a hotel room, of course. Don't you think, Emily? We don't want to impose. I —"

Emily huffed. "Peter, since you seem to get along so fabulously with *that* — with Ralph — perhaps you could share a room."

Peter did not dignify his sister's barb with a response.

Bruno searched his guests' faces, hoping for a softening, a change of heart, but none was forthcoming. Emily and Schlocker had clearly dug in. He could see that to fight would only exacerbate the situation or — *God forbid!* — perhaps even extend the guests' unwanted visit.

He glanced at Virginia and Elizabeth, who bowed their heads in mock modesty. While excited by the drama unfolding about the table, they knew enough to listen quietly.

"Oh," Bruno said. "I suppose we might be able to..." Ironically it was the girls' good behavior that worried him the most. They were... too calm and dainty, their faces pulled in tight, angelic masks. Bruno read the signs and backtracked. "No. No. It's impossible. We're not equipped for guests. It's simply too dangerous."

Schlocker and Emily exchanged a suspicious glance, Emily

having decided not long after crossing the threshold that this entire "family" must be a put-on. Everything was a bit too strange, too on-the-nose. "And why is that?" she demanded.

"Oh, miss…" Bruno said. "I simply meant that the building is old. The wood is rotting and one should know one's way about in the dark."

"Nonsense!" Emily snorted. "Next thing we know, you'll be telling us the house is haunted." She eagle-eyed Schlocker who took the hint to join her in chuckling.

"Oh, no," Bruno replied. "Not at all. It's nothing … like that." Bruno rose from his chair and shuffled his weight from left to right, which served only to further Emily's suspicions.

Peter jumped in with a characteristically lame attempt to steer the conversation into lighter territory. "He means they're vampires, of course!"

Anne took the cue. "Yes. And werewolves."

Peter's eyes lit up. "Wait a minute! Are you a horror fan, too, Miss Morse?"

"Oh, yes. I love them all. Frankenstein… Dracula…"

Peter jumped back in. "And the Mummy!"

"Oh, I love the Mummy," Anne exclaimed. She curled her hands into the shape of gnarled claws. "The way he walks. *Step-scrape, step-scrape, step-scrape!*"

Bruno watched the entire scene with a sort of melancholy longing. But Schlocker quickly brought the conversation back to earth, shooting Anne a scolding frown that quieted her. Bruno threw in one last contribution to their game. "Don't you know?" he asked. "There'll be a full moon tonight!"

"That's perfect!" Peter exclaimed.

"It is an old house," Bruno added. "It's quite dark at night here, far as we are from the road. And there are a lot of noises."

Anne dropped her head, the truth being that the thought of staying in the spooky house had sent a shock of fear sprinting down her spine. Werewolves or no, there was something unsettling that hung over Merrye House, the air of dark secrets.

"Don't say it like that, Bruno. I'm easily startled. Honestly, Mr. Schlocker, I'd rather not stay here, if it's all the same to you."

Emily had lost the last thread of patience and cut in to settle things. "As I see it, Bruno mentioned that there are only two rooms, so, Peter, do you think if you took the car you might find lodgings for Miss Morse?"

Bruno's stiff shoulders fell with relief. "There is an inn in the village. It's not far."

"I do remember seeing a motel," Peter said.

"Fine, fine," Schlocker said. "You just be sure to get her back first thing in the morning, young man. She's a busy day of work ahead, you know."

"Why, sure, no trouble at all," Peter replied, flashing a million watt smile.

Anne's face flushed crimson. She dipped her head to hide her embarrassment. "Thank you, Mr. Howe. That's very kind of you."

"Then, it's settled." Emily left no room for debate.

Bruno had fully thrown in the towel. He addressed Virginia and Elizabeth. "Children, some of our guests are going to stay the night. We'll need to prepare their rooms." The girls' expressions were unchanged and Ralph stared ahead blankly. "Come along, Elizabeth. Virginia, you can take care of the guests while we straighten up."

Elizabeth rose from her seat, obedient. She stuck her tongue out at Virginia, who returned the gesture. "Yes, Bruno," the girls replied in unison.

As the other guests rose from their seats, Emily startled, hands to her heart, hopping back from the table with such force as to nearly topple her chair. She pointed at her white napkin, accusatory, her mouth opening and closing like a dying fish — rendered, for once in her life, silent by terror.

"Ms. Howe, whatever is the matter?" Bruno asked, jumping from his chair to assist.

She sputtered and shrieked, but still nothing coherent came out. Anne, Schlocker and Peter joined Emily in pushing away from the table. While they kept their alert eyes trained on that white napkin, Virginia, Elizabeth and Ralph merely chewed their food, shooting the occasional sideward glance in the direction of the offending linen.

Then, Emily let out an ear-piercing shriek of *"S-s-spider!"*

Nearly simultaneously, Virginia cried. "Winifred!"

Quick-thinking, Schlocker took up the soup bowl and slammed it — *whack* — down on the top of the spider. "Got 'im!" he shouted.

Emily shuddered. "Spiders! Ugh. I hate them!"

Virginia's face went dark with horror. She stared at the soup bowl, muttering to herself. "Bruno says it's not nice to hate…"

Bruno rose from his seat, clocking Virginia's shocked reaction, but unsure of what to do. He stammered and clutched the edge of his table, reaching for words that did not come.

Virginia's moment passed. She turned to Uncle Peter in hopes of commiseration. "We have lots of spiders in this house. Do you like spiders, Mr. Howe?" She flashed him a Mona Lisa grin that soothed Bruno's frayed nerves.

"Sure, Virginia," Peter replied. "I think spiders are great."

Bruno visibly relaxed. "Well then, shall we adjourn to the sitting room?"

"Uncle Peter, I can show you my spiders…" Virginia said.

"Oh well, that would be swell. How about tomorrow?"

Virginia's nod of enthusiasm set Bruno to worrying again.

Peter ushered Anne ahead of him. She gave him an awkward bow of thanks and followed Bruno with some trepidation, into the dark drawing room.

Virginia stopped to release Ralph from his chair. He squat-hopped up onto the table and dug his bare hands into the bony remains of the roast. Virginia laughed and swatted Ralph's hand away.

"Come on, Ralphie. We have to go with Bruno!"

Ralph dug his face into the dish's crispy rib cage and shook it back and forth before coming up for air. He shot Virginia a hangdog look and took her extended hand to jump to the floor.

"Oh, Ralph. You are incorrigible..." Virginia scraped her brain for the right word. "Incorrupt."

Bruno circled back behind Virginia, taking her wrist. "Go on, Ralph," he said, as he pulled Virginia smartly into the hall and shoved her at the stairs.

He turned to Peter and forced a subservient smile. "I'm terribly sorry that we couldn't accommodate all of you, Mr. Howe, Ms. Morse. But we will look forward to seeing you again in the morning."

Peter's head was elsewhere, his eyes trained on Anne, who said, "Oh, yes. I would have loved to stay."

Her words broke his spell. "Me, too. Bruno, but I understand. Goodnight, kids." He waved to Virginia and Elizabeth, who now stood beside each other, one to each step like dolls on a shelf.

Virginia waved at Peter. "Goodnight, Uncle Peter."

Bruno joined the girls on the stairs, hoping that the guests would take the hint. Peter, for one, did. "Oh, yes. We ought to be getting an early start, Miss Morse."

Peter offered Anne his elbow and she wrapped her arm around his. "Yes, I'd like that very much, Mr. Howe."

Chapter Fourteen

Schlocker's eyes were wide with interest and horror; he could not tear himself away. He watched as Ralph placed the remains of the decimated roast's skeleton on the dumbwaiter. He cranked it down, taking great delight in the sound of the gears, until it disappeared into the darkness below.

Sauntering to the door, Peter and Anne were stopped by Emily's words. "Oh, Peter dear. You will need the car keys, won't you?"

Peter turned back, sheepish. She dangled the keys before Peter, who snatched them out of her hand. "Yes, sister dear," he said. "I suppose I will. See you in the morning then. Goodnight, Schlocker. See you in the morning…"

Schlocker did not respond. He stared, dead ahead, at Ralph, who had lost interest in the dumbwaiter and was now crouched in a corner with a bug. He clapped his hands around the bug, encasing it, shouting something that sounded like "peekaboo!" with each rediscovery.

Peter called out to him again. "Schlocker?"

This time, the trance was broken. "Oh. Good night. See you in the morning. Of course." All this was said with his eyes glued to Ralph's every move.

Ralph returned to his beloved dumbwaiter. He leaned the top half of his body into it and placed his ear to the wall, listening.

Suddenly, he noticed Schlocker's attention and, excited, pointed down into the shaft to share his interesting discovery. He bounded across the floor to land at Schlocker's feet, gesturing toward the dumbwaiter and pulling on the man's ill-fitting pants. He grinned at the lawyer, who turned away, hoping to catch someone — anyone — else's eye.

Emily gestured to him and he pulled away from Ralph to follow her into the adjoining sitting room where they huddled together to exchange conspiratorial glances. Schlocker took a cigar from the endless supply that sprouted from his vest pocket like magician's handkerchiefs and grinned at Emily.

"Are you thinking what I'm thinking?" she asked. "This has to be the phoniest setup I have ever seen."

Schlocker dabbed the air with his cigar. "There is something very funny going on here alright! And I intend to find out what it is." He took a draw on his cigar and rakishly cocked his head to let the smoke exit, his attempt at the appearance of a refined gentleman.

* * *

Peter closed Anne's door with a flourish and walked around to slide into the driver's seat beside her. He poked around the steering wheel, angling to find the ignition in the growing darkness. "My goodness," he exclaimed. "I don't think they believe in outdoor lighting around here."

Finding the ignition, he revved up the car and turned, readying to back up. He paused, a sheepish grin spilling across his face. "Um... Miss Morse..."

She smiled back, an equally sheepish look. "Yes?"

"Well, I was thinking that... it's still early. Perhaps you

would like to, uh, have a drink at that inn that Bruno mentioned?"

Anne nodded, pure enthusiasm overtaking her face. "I'd like that very much, Mr. Howe. And maybe a sandwich too, if you don't mind."

Peter chuckled and rubbed his stomach, miming hunger. They were both all smiles — and sighs of relief! — as Peter backed the car up, its headlights illuminating the dead mistletoe draped trees that flanked the dark shape of Merrye House.

Chapter Fifteen

Merrye House stood stark in the moonlight, pregnant with horror. The light in the lower drawing room window went out, throwing the entire downstairs into shadows. Another light flipped on in an upstairs window.

Behind the curtains, Emily marched about the room examining each nook and cranny. It was, by all appearances, a girl's room, every surface of it swathed in dusty pink. Doilies and porcelain trinket boxes and tiny glass figurines, all in pastels. It was enough to make Emily gag. She *harrumphed* as she picked through a pile of costume jewelry. She eagle eyed the room. There was something so strange about it, something beyond the creep chills she got from the1920s era knick-knacks and teddy bears staring her down.

Convinced there was something of value — "There must be!" she muttered — she continued her search, digging through a corner pile of stuffed animals, many of which sported cuts and gouges, perhaps the victims of a child's mangled surgical procedure.

Emily slumped onto the edge of the unmade bed. It sagged beneath even her slight weight. Through the large opening in the doorframe, she could make out a glint of hallway light. A rusty chain lock, which by the look of its one remaining nail may not be there for long, was all that stood between her and the creaking innards of Merrye House.

A sound, a low grunt, echoed down the long hallway. Emily shuddered. "Oh, that filthy little animal!" she exclaimed. She said it loudly enough that anyone outside the door might have heard it, and would have happily admitted that it gave her a little bit of a thrill to know it. *Let them hear me*, she thought.

Considering the limited options the room presented for barricading the door, she tested out the weight of the peeling-pink dresser, throwing her arms about one side and tipping it. A palm sized glass dog figurine slid off its doily bed and to the floor with a loud clunk, which Emily summarily ignored. It would have to do.

She wrestled with the piece of furniture, grabbing hold of its rough edges to drag it five feet to the door, the chunky carved legs carved wide scratches into the polished wooden flooring.

Emily smirked at her own ingenuity. Feeling for the first time all day a modicum of privacy with her own thoughts, she slumped down into an overstuffed velvet chair.

The dimness of the room, lit only by a primitive — and highly flammable by appearance — oil lamp, lulled her into sleepiness. Her eyelids fluttering, she let out a dramatic yawn and stood back up to stretch her arms this way and that.

She pulled off her crisp suit jacket. She moved to drape it over the chair but, thinking better of it, folded it neatly at the foot of the bed, atop her purse. She stood back from the chair, as if it were contagious, and smacked her hand down on the armrest, releasing a powdery cloud of dust. "Oh, this place!"

She retrieved her purse to fish out a tissue and wiped the long surface of the dresser to rest her jacket upon, before peeling off her silk blouse, stockings and skirt. Her undergarments were frilly, a black slip with lacy bits and ornate embroidery that encircled her bosom, and beneath that matching panties, all of it designed to show off her hourglass figure.

Of course, it had been some time since the infinitely unpleasable Emily had been with a man, or a woman for that matter — she wasn't entirely prurient after all! No, she had chosen these underthings for her own appreciation.

She'd often stood in front of her mirror, admiring her features — the delicate arch of her neck, the way the muscles in her thighs barely flexed with each step. She unbounded her tight updo to shake out a headful of ashy blond curls that fell about her shoulders.

As she twirled before the mirror, a glittering object in the wide-open closet caught her eye. Perhaps there was something of value there after all. Emily abandoned the mirror with visions of jewels dancing through her imagination. She was disappointed to discover it was nothing more than a glittery bit of fabric, the shelves stuffed with nothing more than the same cheap antique trinkets the house seemed to be overflowing with.

But in the interest of finding something, anything, that would make this entire doomed excursion worth her time, she pulled out hangars to examine the items of clothing. Most were simple shift dresses, ridiculously outdated with their childlike shapes and patterns. But — aha! — here was that bit of sparkle, a lacy negligee out of *Sunset Boulevard*. Her fingers grazed over the plush black fur that lined the oversized cuffs. Emily turned to the mirror, holding the negligee up to her body.

* * *

A door shrouded in darkness opened to the warm orange light of the oil lamp that heralded Elizabeth's entry. She turned to her own shadow, cast bigger than life upon the wall and giggled, holding her finger up to shush the both of them.

She wore a simple '20s style nightgown bedecked with the

same type of ditsy flower pattern that permeated the bedroom that Emily now slept in. She frowned thinking about that woman — *that terrible woman* — in her bed! If Elizabeth thought about it too long, she would get terribly angry, so she had resolved to do as Bruno so often advised her and "think happy thoughts!"

Elizabeth shook the anger off and peeked down the darkened corridor. "Virginia?" she called out to the shadows. She did not dare to venture further on her own; unlike Virginia, Elizabeth had never been fond of the stuffed birds that lined the hallway, peeking out from carved nooks and branches and even hanging from the ceiling. She had always hated the way they were posed, as if frozen in mid-flight. "Virginia!" she called again.

There was no answer, so Elizabeth stepped forward, trepidatious. She held the light far ahead of her, training her gaze on the floor. She passed one doorway, then another and —

"Boo!"

Virginia popped out from a corner lurking spot to frighten her sister. Elizabeth could not help but jump back. With her arms raised high above her head, the hands formed into curled claws, Virginia's shadow resembled a gnarled witch.

Elizabeth frowned. "Shush, Virginia! You're going to get us in trouble. Where are you going?"

"I'm going to kiss Daddy goodnight!" Virginia replied, as if it were the only possible answer. Virginia snatched the oil lamp from Elizabeth and crossed in front of her to head toward the stairs. As she did so, she whispered into her sister's ear. "Are you scared?"

Elizabeth spun around. *Scared? Never!* "Scared of what?" she said.

"You know. Those people."

"I'm not scared of them," Elizabeth replied. "I hate them."

Virginia's lips curled at the edges. She tried so hard to be good, to hide her displeasure with things for Bruno's sake. She so hated to see Bruno disappointed. But she could not help herself sometimes.

"You're not supposed to hate..." she replied, unconvincingly.

"Well," Elizabeth said. "You should hate them too. They don't like spiders, remember?"

Virginia's faux demureness melted away with the mention of her spiders. "I know he does. Do you know what? That man looks just like a big fat bug, doesn't he?" She covered her mouth to stifle a giggle but it only served to distort the sound, the off-kilter lilt of madness.

"She certainly does. He looks like a big bug. Maybe a cockroach!" Elizabeth clapped her hands together.

The two girls bounced off each other's energy, their giggles growing more manic, their voices rising.

"You know what I'd like to do?" Virginia asked.

"I think I do know!" Elizabeth exclaimed. "Is it really fun playing *Spider*?"

Virginia raised her arms, the one with the lantern and the other empty, and crossed them in front of her face just as she had those sharp knives. She sawed the invisible knives, her spider appendages back and forth, throwing contorted shadows across the menagerie of stuffed birds that looked over them.

"Playing *Spider* is the most fun in the world!"

Chapter Sixteen

Virginia eased the door open with a creak. As the darkness before her split with the shaft of light from her oil lamp, she turned down the flame and whispered, "Sorry, daddy. I'm coming to tuck you in."

She tippy-toed to set her lamp atop the bedside table and sat herself at the foot of the stained quilt that outlined the lumpy shape of a person. A striped pajama-clad elbow was crooked up at a strange angle, balanced against a pillow. Virginia smiled tenderly at the faceless figure and leaned in closer.

"Daddy, are you playing hide-and-seek again?"

Virginia giggled and pulled the edge of the quilt down, slowly to reveal – first, a clump of brittle black hair, then a fold of leathery skin, and finally, the pitch black of empty eye sockets. She lifted the mummified corpse's chin, sending the bottom jaw sliding slack toward the back of the skull and kissed the rotten thing's forehead.

"Nighty-night, daddy!"

She tucked the blankets in around her daddy's shoulders and lifted herself from the bed. She took up her oil lamp and headed toward the door.

The shaft of light narrowed as she inched open the door to

slip out. She stopped, turning one more time to blow a kiss and shut the door, leaving the body shrouded in darkness.

Virginia disappeared into her shared room. As she shut her door, at the other end of the dark hallway, another door opened.

The movement was stealthy, just a crack at first. The tips of black-gloved fingers appeared. They crawled around the door jamb, followed by the shadowy outline of a figure who pulled the door shut behind him. The figure, a man, flinched at the sound of the door latch clicking into its frame and pressed itself tight against the wall.

The man fumbled with a metal flashlight, clicking its switch back and forth. When no light was forthcoming, the man hit the light in his palm, then used both hands to forcibly push the power switch. It clicked and popped, releasing a circle of light.

Although his face was well-hidden within the torch's sickly yellow glow, there was no mistaking the man's identity. Schlocker's tongue shot out to feel around the butt of the extinguished cigar hanging from the corner of his mouth. His eyes darted back and forth, down the corridor, more as a matter of nervousness than of caution. After all, he thought, what could Bruno possibly do to him even if he were to be discovered?

He shaded the torch like a burglar, imagining himself a figure in one of the crime films he so loved. An *international cat burglar* perhaps, convinced in the way that only truly mediocre men generally are, that he would have excelled at any task he chose. He pressed himself into the wall with the *Get Smart* theme song playing in the back corridors of his brain, and inched down the hallway.

The beam of his light rose and fell to pick out the shapes of the stuffed birds that lined the wall. He settled it upon one particularly disturbing creature, a one-eyed condor posed in mid-meal, the resin-shiny corpse of a picked-apart rat in repose at its feet.

"Where the hell are the goods?" More puzzled than

anything, he dropped the beam, unpeeled himself from the wall and continued down the hallway. The light beam picked out a doorknob. By the look of the corroded brass and the cobwebs surrounding the frame, it was obvious that it had been closed for some time. "Aha!"

He listened at each door in turn, slinking toward that last one. He'd already decided that, should a door fly open, it'd be easy enough to explain his presence as a late night bathroom run, but he wasn't keen to try it out.

He raised a hand to wipe the string of slobber that had gathered around his disintegrating cigar butt. He had reached it — *the* door. He knew, and he could not have told you why, being a man who eschewed all esoterica, simply... knew... that something of great interest lay behind that door.

Of great *value*, he corrected himself. He'd already played out the possibilities in his mind, had been for the two weeks that passed since Emily had called him with a story about the Merrye Family fortune.

What if he did find the mother lode there, without Emily? He had pondered that, too. He certainly did not feel any moral compunction to share the news — or the loot — with Emily, who would inherit the house and the bank accounts and god-knows-what-else.

No, if he were to discover a treasure, he'd pocket it away, knowing full well that if he didn't, Emily would kick him out on his keister with nothing more than his measly barrister fee.

Schlocker stood before the door, listening in the darkness. His gloved hand twisted the doorknob; it groaned at his touch. He pushed inward. The door squeaked, opened a few more inches and stopped cold. He jiggled the knob and, when that yielded no results, shoved the whole of his squat strength into the door. It pushed in further, then halted, as if blocked by a rolled carpet. With enough room to weave his arm inside, Schlocker wriggled in further still till his head and shoulder were firmly in the opening.

At once, he recoiled, repelled by an odd and decidedly unpleasant sensation. His arms went akimbo, searching and swimming. It was as if his upper body had slidden into the clutches of a room-sized cobweb!

He swatted, frantic, to shake off the unidentified sticky substance. Finally, he stepped forward to push through it. He shook his head and clawed at the strings that clung to his pajama top.

As his arms swung to and fro, the circular light of his torch happened upon a swiftly-moving shape! There, on the floor! The thing, a palm sized creature scuttled away in its strange side-to-side gait.

Schlocker gulped. He followed the creature's path with his torch, lighting its way to the furthest corner of the room. Schlocker squinted at the shape, struggling to connect the bits and pieces of the horror before him into some type of coherent picture... there was blood... a good deal of it! It spread across the floor in splats and spots. A trail of it, crispy with age, streaked across the floor as if a mouse-sized body were dragged.

Schlocker wanted to turn away. He wanted to run back to his room and bolt the door. But he was compelled by the very strangeness of it all. He steadied his shaking hands and leaned down, closer to the floor, training his light where —

A fuzzy, palm-sized spider tore into the top of what appeared to be a hefty supply of eviscerated rat carcasses.

Schlocker backed away, sickened. His hand flew to his mouth, his stubby cigar dropping to the floor. And still he did not run from the sight. Trapped by the sheer horror, all he could do was stare.

The silence was punctuated with the spider's crunches and clicks. Schlocker swung the torch about the room. He was shocked to discover several similar piles of rodents — chipmunk, squirrel, rat — bones and organs and bits scattered about the room. Atop each pile, another of the tarantulas dug in.

The spiders chattered and slipped out of the light, hiding themselves in the darkest corners, beneath the lowest rats.

Schlocker swung his flashlight up the wall and to the ceiling beams, where a short row of fruit bats dangled upside down! They fluttered and chattered in reaction to the light.

And that was that. The sight of those glowing eyes, the bodies tensing in response to the light, broke him from his horror trance and he alighted from the room, slamming the door shut behind him.

Back in the hallway, surrounded by those dread stuffed birds, Schlocker panted and reassessed. He could run, he thought. Abscond to the room and none would be the wiser.

He paused, seriously considering it. Then, he shook it off, gathered his nerve and carried on. Having endured such a manner of horrible things, Schlocker again found his desire to locate the mysterious Merrye treasure growing. His obsession led him past the wall of birds toward the stairs. He moved in slow spurts, pausing to listen for movement.

Schlocker reached the bottom of the stairs and trained his light on the opposite end of the hall, the door that opened into the drawing room. As he approached, he felt the cold chill of a stranger's stare at his back. He spun on heel, the yellow circle reflected in the dead gray eye of *yet another stuffed bird!*

Shaking his head, he entered the drawing room, moving along the room's perimeter. The number of birds he'd encountered by now was positively absurd. So much so, that he wondered if the grounds didn't house some sort of aviary he had missed.

One by one, he ticked off the names in his head — *egret (or was that an ocelot? Or maybe an ocelot was more like a gazelle?), flamingo, eagle...*

Having circled the entire octagon-shaped room, the last of the birds was an owl, posed with a mouse flopping from its beak, its yellow eyes seemingly lit from within. Schlocker drew closer and the thing emitted a piercing shriek! It extended its wings with a great beating of air, the mouse carcass dropping to the floor below.

Schlocker's arms flew up, reflexive. But the owl settled back into its perch, taking no interest in the man, who gathered himself and continued his search. He passed by the dumbwaiter, stopping at the closed roll top desk. "Bingo!" he exclaimed.

He set the light atop the smooth desk back and gave a few tugs on the rolltop handle. He was surprised to see it open, the momentum pulling it up a few inches. Excited at the possibilities that lie in wait, he felt an unfamiliar surge of guilt.

But curiosity quickly overpowered the passing feeling and he slid the top the rest of the way open, revealing a series of pigeonholes, each stuffed with odds and ends. It was, he noted, a shockingly ordinary assortment of items — pencil nubs, receipts, scraps of tickets and grocery lists, envelopes.

He withdrew a few of the more official-looking papers to better examine them in the light. Seeing that the papers were nothing more than junk mail, he quickly lost interest, instead turning his gaze to a squarish object in the far corner of the desk.

He handled the item — a book-sized box — turning it over in his hand, searching for the opening. At last, he found a catch, which he flipped open to reveal a small drawer. Having set the flashlight down, he squinted into the sparse bit of light it cast from afar, struggling to make out the unfamiliar shape of the object in his hand.

He reached inside and withdrew a soft object. The shape was odd and wholly unrecognizable to his fingers. He held it up, closer to his face, his other hand grabbing for the flashlight. As the light hit the object, he reeled back, dropping a *human ear* onto the desk.

Schlocker dropped the flashlight. He rubbed his hands together, frantic, as if washing his gloves with invisible soap.

Pull it together, man! There must be some reasonable explanation. Why, it could be a prop... or a plant. Yes, it was put here specifically to scare them off the trail of the real fortune that was surely planted somewhere nearby!

Although he did not entirely buy his own story, it was plausible enough that he could pluck up the courage to place the half-mummified bit of flesh back in its box. He stowed it back in its pigeonhole and closed the rollertop. *Out of sight, out of mind.*

As he turned to go, it occurred to him that he had acted too hastily. After all, what better way to hide something than to plant that *clearly fake* ear. *Why, I must be on the right track then!*

Ample helpings of both curiosity and greed sent him back to the roll-top desk, which he flipped open for one last peek. He thrust his hand inside of one of the deep wooden pigeon holes and grimaced. He was feeling around inside, when a sound stopped him cold.

He cocked his head and withdrew his arm, switching off the flashlight. It sounded like the closing of a door, followed by light footsteps. Schlocker's heart dropped, his breath caught in the cage of his chest. He closed the rollertop, oh-so-quietly, oh-so-quickly and pressed himself into the corner space between the wall and the oversized desk.

A spill of light illuminated the hallway, followed by Bruno. Schlocker watched him proceed, lamp in hand, down the hallway and out the front door. He peeped over the top of the desk.

From that vantage point, he could follow Bruno's movements through the front window. The light of his lamp danced around the porch before passing off into the distance. It was hard to tell how far away he was through the translucent layer of window dust.

Schlocker fussed with the collar of his pajamas as if

smoothing out a suit coat. He stood up and having regained his fortitude, resolved to search the rolltop desk. But before he could even get the top up, another sound grabbed his attention. This one came from the dumbwaiter.

Schlocker's head turned, as if of its own accord, toward the vague shuffling sound coming from that dreaded apparatus.

He moved, crouching, toward its impenetrably dark opening and leaned his head inside to listen. The sound presented itself again, clearer and louder, a restless shuffling and beneath that...

Is that moaning? Schlocker straightened himself up, withdrawing his head. This was so much worse than he thought, he'd mused. Why they probably have some poor schmucks tied up down in that basement!

Suddenly hyper aware of his body — the shuddering, the goosebumps — he tongued the mushy pile that was his cigar, pushing it to the other corner of his mouth.

There it was again. That moaning sound! It emanated from the far corners of the pantry adjacent to the dumbwaiter. Schlocker convinced himself that he was going to explore in the name of helping whatever poor soul was trapped in the house of horrors. But in reality, it was nothing more than base morbid curiosity that propelled him forward. He willed himself to move, pushing through the dusty pantry toward the door at the other end. He rested his face against the wood, listening. *"Ohhhhhhh, unggggg..."* the sounds came. Schlocker gripped the doorknob but before he could turn it, the door latch clicked open. The door swung inward with an audible groan.

Schlocker harkened to the sounds that issued from that space beyond the door. He felt his way along the wall, descended stairs that groaned beneath his weight. He shaded his torch, only lighting the steps directly in front of his feet. He took it slow, watching each foot land, one then the other.

With the ever present danger of structural collapse looming

over him, the stairway descent seemed to be taking an extraordinarily long time! He sighed with relief as he reached the solid concrete at the bottom of the steps.

He blinked, his eyes adjusting to the unfamiliar surroundings. The basement was dark, with spots of light here and there emanating from single light bulbs spread about the ceiling. They weren't doing much, so Schlocker cast his torch around.

He took his time, examining objects as he marched the room's perimeter. To say that he was disappointed would be an understatement. His fingers traced the outlines of a neglected laundry area with a long drainboard, a stack of rusty washboards, and a stained sink.

Beyond the laundry, he spotted — *no, that couldn't be right!* — a row of coffins! Five to be exact The wooden toe pinchers in tight formation. Schlocker shook his head in disbelief. For a brief second, it did occur to him that he had read an article about how expensive funerals were. Perhaps this was the treasure? Coffins?!

His curiosity would not allow him to ignore this strange sight. He approached the first box and swiped at it to release a blanket of dust. He leaned in tight, his nose nearly touching the blank brass nameplate affixed to its front.

An urge overtook him, and he lifted his hand and rapped on the wooden box. The sound that greeted him was solid, rather than hollow. Schlocker pulled back and slowly, a smile spread across his face. It grew so wide that the shreds that were once a cigar tumbled to the ground.

But Schlocker seemed to not notice the loss. He shook his head wryly and muttered to himself, "Well, aren't you sly?" What better place to hide valuables than in a coffin?

He pried at the lid of the first coffin, noting that while it appeared to be securely nailed shut, it was also oddly warped. It was in this warping, Schlocker realized, this slight outward curling of the wood around the edges that one could — if he were enterprising enough, shove something inside and pry the lid off.

He hunched the torch under his armpit, both hands skimming the edges of the wooden box in search of the best way in. There was one spot, in the upper right corner, where the warping had left a space large enough for him to slip the tips of two fingers inside. "Aha!" He turned on heel to search for something to pry with.

As he spun, the torch beneath his arms played out over a wall full of gardening tools. Schlocker moved in, excited at the menagerie of sharp instruments at his disposal. He'd always believed that, at heart, man was violent and would jump at the chance to stab something given half a chance.

He took up the largest of the tool options, a rusted pitchfork with two missing tines. He turned the pitchfork this way and that, stretching his five-foot-six frame so that he could wiggle the two operational tines into the open crease in the wood. He'd accomplished all thus far with the flashlight still tucked under one arm, but as he shoved the tines further into the wood, the light rolled away, its final location unseen.

Schlocker huffed and puffed, pushing his full weight into the pitchfork's handle. The lid's corner burst open with an audible pop. Schlocker was assaulted with a face full of corpse dust that sent him reeling back. He waved his arms, coughing, as he turned in circles searching for his lost flashlight.

When, at last, he spotted the light's beaming circle and leaned down toward it, he realized — too late — that he was tottering at the edge of a pit. The beam of light issuing from somewhere far below illuminated what happened next.

A pair of hands, so matted with filth and fur that they could scarcely be described as human, reached from the shadowy hole to grab Schlocker's ankle! As the creature clawed at the cuffs of his pajamas, another set of hands joined the assault, the sounds of the two creatures' wild cries like feral hogs.

Schlocker twisted, kicking at the errant limbs to free himself and falling backward on his ass in the process. The creatures cried out, a mournful howl.

Safe from the hands — for it had now become clear that the animals were contained in a sort of pit — Schlocker inched forward, ever so slowly. He stood up, a few feet from the edge, and peered down into the flashlight-lit confines of their domain.

Schlocker had to blink several times to convince himself that what he was seeing was, indeed, real for the creatures below did not fit anywhere in his deeply-proscribed and quite practical view of reality.

There were two that he could see well, one a man — inasmuch as he could be called one. He was upright, on two feet, and had facial features that were arranged in the vague shape of a human face, but that was as far as the resemblance went. His body was stooped and squat, with limbs that pointed at strange angles, the fingers elongated, tipped with thick yellow claws.

The snarling, hoary woman beside him — she was discernible as female only for the drooping breast-like appendages that swung in and out of her makeshift rag dress with her movements — was even more pitiful, in that she had clearly made an attempt at braiding the thin hairs that grew long from her scalp.

For perhaps the first time in his life, Schlocker had been struck silent. He took the scene in, the man and woman with their pitiful howls and beyond them, their filth-encrusted surroundings.

Discarded bones and bits of gore were strewn about the earthen floor and the walls were covered in bloody claw marks.

The pit-dwellers raised their hands to him and the woman hissed loudly, a sound so otherworldly, it pulled Schlocker from his fear-induced stupor. Without a word or a sound, the man turned and ran, darkness to damned, toward the safety of the stairs.

Dayna Noffke

His shin collided with the bottom step and he cried out, just as the door above swung open. The sigh of relief had barely escaped his lips before it died too.

Chapter Seventeen

When Virginia had suggested to Elizabeth that the two of them sneak down to the basement that night, it was nothing out of the ordinary. The girls delighted in visiting Aunt Clara and Uncle Ned, a joy that was regularly denied them by Bruno.

On such occasions, Virginia would throw out a pouty lip, insistent that they should be able to see their aunt and uncle. But Bruno held firm on this one issue. He was the only one who should visit the basement abode.

Two years before, Virginia had awakened her sister, oil lamp in hand to suggest that they "creep down to the basement," and once they had done so undetected, it became a regular game of theirs.

Once they were certain that Bruno had retired, the girls would arm themselves with an oil lamp and a fistful of dinner leftovers, often nothing more than bits of meat gristle secreted into their dinner napkins, and traverse the path to the basement. On the rare occasion that Ralph attempted to join them, they would wave him off like a pesky fly.

The girls doted on Ned and Clara, treating them as pets; they would slide down into the pit, petting them and brushing their coarse hair as aunt and uncle tore into their snacks.

On this night, Virginia and Elizabeth had come down to the basement armed with a hairbrush and the few spindly roast bones they had pilfered from the evening's trash.

As the girls opened the door, their eyes went wide with delight at the sight of Schlocker, huddled over, rubbing his sore shin. Hunched over the bottom step, he bolted up, throwing his hands in front of him in a sort of surrender stance.

"Now, look here! This just won't do. I don't know what you are up to right now, but this has gone far enough. Ladies, please. I just need to…"

There was no reply. To Schlocker the girls appeared as ghosts, a haunting and unmoving vision of terror. In reality, Virginia was doing her best not to break into a giggle fit — the sight of a grown man stammering and shaking so never failed to elicit such a reaction.

Their quiet unnerving him further, Schlocker pivoted his head as if searching for escape, for his flashlight, for anything! His panic grew. There was no place to run and his flashlight lay in the depths of the pit behind him with whatever-those-creatures-were…

"Yes. This is beyond the bounds of prudence!" Schlocker changed tactics, drawing himself up to his courtroom posture. He took a few breaths, steadying his voice. "Yes, beyond the bounds of good taste. I do not know what sort of things are going on in this family but I fully intend to get to the bottom of it!"

Virginia's eyes darted to the side to gauge her sister's reaction. Elizabeth caught her gaze and grabbed on to her hand. Still, they did not speak.

They took one step down. One step closer…

"I… I didn't want to do this, but I'm afraid that I'm going to have to call in the authorities! There are laws… criminal laws, I might add… to cover things like this…"

The girls took another wordless step down.

Schlocker could no longer hide his panic. His breath caught

in his throat. He alighted to the corner of the room. There was no escaping, but it was the most distance he could get in the cramped quarters.

He squeezed his eyes shut tight against the horrors, listening to the creaks that signaled the girls' slow descent toward him. Had he looked up then, he would have seen how Virginia's face morphed from girlish to fiendish, her eyes darkening as if possessed. He would have seen Elizabeth toss the treat bones to the snarling pit creatures. All of this as they tippy-toed closer, ever closer to Schlocker.

When he could sense them drawing, the warmth of the oil lamp, their breath steaming in the chill air, he opened his mouth in one last attempt at saving himself. "Girls... what is that you wa—"

A wave of nausea washed over him when Virginia produced, from behind her back, her serrated knives.

A trickle of piss inched down Schlocker's pajama pants.

"Ew!" Elizabeth screeched, pointing at the puddle forming around his foot.

Virginia gingerly lifted her foot, moving it a few inches out of the liquid's way. She crossed the knives in front of her chest, sawing them back and forth in an x. She delighted in this part — something about the clinking of the knives. With a terrible cry, Virginia leapt upon Schlocker, knives flashing forward. The weight and ferocity of her attack slammed the man to the floor. He scrambled sideways, trapped against the wall. Elizabeth alighted behind them. She pried the discarded pitchfork free of the coffin.

Virginia's excitement had given way to carelessness, allowing Schlocker to slip partially free He ducked beneath her, her knife nicking the shoulder seam of his pajama, and ran for the stairs with Virginia clinging to his back like some hell-bound equestrian.

As Schlocker scrambled up the stairs on hands and knees,

Virginia flailed, hanging on tight. Her knives rose and fell, digging into the tender meat of his neck and scalp.

Schlocker's energy was waning, the pain slowing his movements to a crawl. He flipped over to face Virginia, throwing his arms up by means of protection. But Virginia hacked and slashed all the faster, as if in the throes of a supernatural fit.

Ever a barrister, Schlocker cried out in a last ditch effort to sway the girls. "No! No! This isn't right! There are proper procedures. Judicial procedures!"

Virginia paused, cocking her head to examine with interest a flap of scalp that had fallen free of Schlocker's head. She poked at it, giggling at the way the skin and hair bounced at her touch.

"These things can be litigated!" he cried.

He lifted his hand to push back the flap of skin, lowering it to see —

Elizabeth, to the side of her sister, the pitchfork raised high above her head.

It was the last thing Schlocker saw.

The last thing he heard was the howling of the pit-creatures, a background to Elizabeth's screams.

"Kill him! Kill him!"

Chapter Eighteen

Ralphie stalked the outer edges of Merrye House's upper level. Despite his stooped posture, or perhaps because of it, he crawled along the eaves with the dexterity of a house cat.

Ralphie had tried, as he often did, to follow Elizabeth and Virginia on their nightly creepings. But, as so often happened, they had shooed him away, telling him he was too little to join in their games.

Even as he crawled upon the roof — his next favorite thing besides playing with his sisters — the memory stung so deeply that he stopped to pout. With his thumb in his mouth and knees drawn up to his hollow chest, from below he gave the appearance of a cathedral gargoyle. Had someone informed Ralph of this, his curious shape, he would have laughed along with them with no real understanding.

No, as Bruno had sadly explained to the doctors earlier that same day, his deterioration seemed to be proceeding at a rate that far outpaced that of his sisters. Ralph's body hair grew long and curly. So long that Bruno shaved it off regularly, lest it draw even more unsightly attention on their trips to the doctor in town. His arms had begun to twist and he stooped forward and to the side. And his craving for flesh… well, that Bruno did not dare share with the doctors, for he knew what came after that.

But on this clear summer night, Ralph was gloriously oblivious to all of this as he enjoyed his little climbing game. His pouting over — indeed, he could not remember why he had stopped at all — he scampered over to hang upside down from one of the eaves.

From this vantage, he could peek into a window. His sisters weren't in their room. He knew this because he had wanted to follow them, after all. But he still grew giddy with the excitement of this forbidden game of his. He loved to peek into their room, and on some nights, he would climb in through the window to drape himself in their frilly dresses and roll around on their pile of pastel quilts.

Ralph lowered himself further, and what he saw was not an empty room, but Emily — decked in gauzy, fur-trimmed robe, sitting at the edge of the bed. She turned toward him, running her hand along the length of her stockings and unfastened her black garters.

Ralph watched with a naive curiosity. He had never noticed the shape of a woman before and was not particularly excited by it. Rather, he wondered… *What was she doing?*

Emily, sensing that spine tingle of being watched, spun to face first the door, then the window. Her eyes met Ralph's where he hung head-down from the roof, an expression of dumb wonderment frozen on his face.

Emily rose from the bed, her face a blank, devoid of emotion. She approached the window, as if doubting the reality of the vision of that creature in the window. As she drew closer, their eyes locked again and Ralph's face broke into a wide open, fang-y smile.

Emily let out an ear-piercing shriek, and fell to the floor in a dead faint.

Chapter Nineteen

Bruno patrolled the hallways. He had tried to get a bit of sleep, having set his alarm to check on things, as was his nightly habit. He'd closed his eyes for the better part of an hour, lying there in silence, even as a hundred possible horrible scenarios ticked through his mind. Finally, in acknowledgment of the uselessness of this endeavor, he rose from the bed.

He thought that, perhaps if he were to check on the girls, he would be assured and could get at least a few hours of shut eye. He pushed all misgivings to the back of his mind. I'm certain they're just fine, he told himself. Everything will be just… fine.

But when he had passed by the room where the girls slept, and popped the door open just a foot's worth, he had seen the empty beds. His heart sank. Worse yet, when he'd run to Ralph's room, he'd found the same — Ralph was gone.

So now, he patrolled the halls, locking his fear tight in his chest. Although he could not stand the man, he hoped for nothing more than to hear Schlocker tromping down the hall, that damn cigar clinging to his dry lips.

So far, Bruno had been met with an unsettling silence. Schlocker's bed was empty, and Bruno feared the worst.

He called out, a sharp whisper, "Virginia! Elizabeth!"

There was no answer.

Bruno peeked his head into door frames as he passed each room. He slid along the walls, his shadow preceding him, to double check the locks on window sashes and doors.

He clocked movement, something in the corner of his eye. Bruno let out a long sigh, his hand shaking slightly at the familiar creaking sound of the grinding dumbwaiter gears, lifting itself from the basement below.

He approached it, his fears confirmed. The crank for the dumbwaiter turned of its own accord, powered by someone below. As the compartment lifted, Bruno saw, first the top of its wooden frame, then, Schlocker's body, stuffed inside. When he was fully visible in the dumbwaiter's opening, Bruno merely stared in silence.

Schlocker's body was stuffed in at a strange angle, folded in on itself, his head hanging upside-down, hanging from the body by a few tenuous strings of sinew.

The dumbwaiter screeched to a halt. Bruno could do nothing more than shake his head in sad resignation. He knew that there was no turning back. He knew what needed to be done.

I must gather the children, he thought.

He walked away, leaving Schlocker's minced body in full view. He stopped short of leaving the room and doubled back to throw a white tablecloth over the corpse, leaving only a dangling arm hanging free in sight.

Chapter Twenty

Bruno took his place at the head of the dinner table and sat with his hands folded before him, the picture of decorum and thoughtfulness. He bowed his head, as if in prayer. In truthfulness, he did not want the children to witness the intense sorrow that had overtaken him.

You must be strong for the children, he reminded himself. He ran the phrase over and over in his mind, the phrase that he had said a hundred times and which had finally come to its fruition.

"I promised Titus that I would take care of the children... and that I would not allow them to be taken and displayed for the public, or sent to an institution. I promised... no matter what," he whispered.

Virginia and Elizabeth were seated around them, each in their respective dinner places. For once, all were dead silent. They sensed Bruno's sadness, but even more-so, were rendered mute by the knowledge that he had discovered their actions. That they had been bad.

Virginia turned to Elizabeth, whispering behind her hand. "Do you think Bruno hates us?"

At last Bruno lifted his head. He held an errant fork, which he tapped on the table, a sort of nervous twitch.

Virginia's eyes overflowed with tears. "Don't hate me, Bruno! Please don't hate me. She made me do it! She made me!" Virginia pointed an accusing finger at her sister.

"He was spying on us!" Elizabeth cried. "He was going to tell on us. He was going to tell Bruno, and then they would take us away from you, wouldn't they?"

Bruno nodded, every patient. Virginia leapt from her chair to kneel beside him. She laid her head against his chest and sobbed freely while Bruno patted her head, murmuring, "There, there. Go and sit down. It's all right now."

Virginia sniffled and returned to her chair, sticking out her tongue at Elizabeth before taking her seat.

"Yes, Elizabeth. You are right. He was going to tell. It's all right, Virginia. I could never hate you. I always knew that it would come to this someday, but... so soon..." Bruno said.

"And you really don't hate us?" Virginia cried.

"I promised your daddy that I would take care of you. I would never, *ever* hate you, Virginia. I would never hate any of you."

"Well, you ought to hate that man. He was going to hurt us," Elizabeth declared.

"Elizabeth, I have told you that it is not nice to hate..." Bruno shuddered, the image of Schlocker's bulging eyes fresh in his gray matter. He righted himself. After all, he had to stay strong for them.

"Now, children, I have something I want to tell you. And you need to listen very carefully." Bruno dropped his fork. He locked eyes with the girls, as they settled in to listen.

"A long, long time ago, I promised your daddy that I would take care of you, both of you girls — and Ralph! That I would take care of you forever. How this — this man, Schlocker — he was mean and nasty. He was going to take you away. All of you! Take you to where old Bruno could never see you again. Well… you've hurt Schlocker now, and he can't do that."

Virginia bowed her head in faux remorse as Bruno continued. "But you see… there will be other Mr. Schlockers, much meaner and much nastier, if you can believe it! And they will come here and take you and Ralph away and you won't be able to hurt those other Schlockers because…"

Bruno's eyes misted over once more. He dropped his head to hide his pain, but a tear slipped out, falling to where he had folded his hands on the table.

"We're so sorry, Mr. Bruno!" Virginia burst out crying.

"Oh, hush!" Elizabeth snarled, slapping Virginia's hand.

"Children, please no fighting. Not now. What I was saying is that we won't be able to stop them again, because there will be too many of them, you understand…"

Virginia wiped her tears on a dinner napkin. Elizabeth looked as if she had been slapped, her face red, eyes wide and frozen. Virginia leapt from her chair to bore herself into Bruno, hugging him tightly. Elizabeth jumped up to join them. The girls clung to him, pitifully.

"I don't want to go away from you, Bruno! They can't make me!" Virginia sobbed.

"No," Bruno replied, peeling the girls back from him. He composed himself, offering them a soft smile. "No of course I won't let them take you. I promised your daddy that I wouldn't."

Elizabeth dove in for another hug. "I knew you wouldn't, Bruno. I'm not afraid!"

When Bruno spoke again, it was more to himself than to the children who hung on his every word. "We didn't have much longer, anyway, did we? Soon, Ralph would have been ready to join Uncle Ned and your Aunt Clara and then… you…"

His words were choked with sorrow. He regretted speaking so in front of Elizabeth and Virginia, but as he pulled back to look at them he sighed with relief. From the looks on their faces, he could tell that nothing he'd said had affected them in the least. They remained painfully naive as to the dreadful position they were now in.

"We want to stay here forever, Bruno. We want to stay with Ralph and Uncle Ned and Daddy and Aunt Clara – and you! You, most of all!"

Elizabeth rested her head on Bruno's shoulder and he patted her hair. "Yes," he replied. "We will. We will – forever and ever. I promise. Now, I have a very big surprise!"

"Yes," Bruno continued. "A big surprise! I know where I can find a nice, new toy. You are going to love it. It does wonderful things! It shines like a star."

Virginia began to wiggle her head and clap with delight and her joy was like balm to her caretaker's frayed nerves.

"And you can stay up late to see it! But I will have to go a little ways to get it for you."

Elizabeth threw out a pouty bottom lip in protest. "Please don't go away, Bruno! I'm scared."

"No, no. Don't be silly. I won't take long, just a few minutes. I'm going to depend on you, Elizabeth. I need you to keep your brother and sister out of trouble while I'm gone. You go and find your brother and keep everyone busy while I'm gone"

Elizabeth nodded her head, excited for the chance to correct Virginia, who despite their difference in age, like to pretend that she was the older sister. "Oh, I will do it!" Elizabeth replied. "I promise, I will keep everyone out of trouble!"

Bruno stood up. As he walked behind the girls, he stopped to give them each a last, filial squeeze.

"I'll be good. I promise," Virginia assured him.

"I'm sure you will," Bruno replied, though his face was dark with worry. You know what you need to do, he thought. Now just steel yourself to it.

* * *

Bruno hurried through the house, up the stairs and to his room, where he gathered up a few items, among them two large pieces of luggage. He juggled the worn leather bags, tucking one under his arm while the other dangled by its handle, dropping first one bag and then the other before he had them properly arranged for transport.

As he passed Emily's door on his way to the stairs, he paused as if to knock. He muttered, considering a few different things to say. In the end, he simply couldn't do it. After all, he thought, he certainly couldn't tell her the truth, now could he?

"Lots of luck, Ms. Howe," he said.

Chapter Twenty-One

Inside the room, the unconscious Emily was entirely unaware of Bruno's presence. Just as unaware as she was of Ralphie, who now sat astride her, his face just a few inches from hers.

He watched Emily with great interest, as if he had discovered a new species and wished to know more. He spun her golden hair between his fingers, rubbing it against his cheek.

Emily's eyelids fluttered as she fought her way back to consciousness. Ralph clapped his hands in delight and stood up, distracted by the sound of Bruno starting up the limousine outside. He ran to the window, pointing at the car.

As Emily came around, the reality of her situation came to her in bits and pieces. First she wondered how she had come to be on the floor, then what this room was, and at last — when she had pieced together that she was at Merrye House, then — she saw Ralph and screamed once more!

She jumped up and ran to the door, fumbling with the dresser that she had placed in front of it. Ralph turned from the window, watching her with that giant fang-toothed grin that so unnerved her.

Emily pushed the dresser as hard as she could. It moved in

fits and starts, carving deep grooves in the wood. Once she had moved it far enough to get the door open a crack, there was still the latch to contend with.

The entire time, Ralph simply watched from his window post. Emily bolted into the hallway and slammed the door behind her. In her normal state, she would have thought things through. She might have gone back in to look for her car keys and taken off on her own.

She could figure out the inheritance later — after all, she was going to get the place no matter how hard they went to scare her off. But she was not her normal self and so she ran... screaming, just like one of those ninny girls in the horror movies. The girls that she despised for their simple ways and shrieking voices.

Emily was now one of those girls. *And so be it!* She thought. *I have to get out of this madhouse!*

The approaching sound — footsteps and girlish giggles — compelled her to flatten her back against the wall. She pushed to gather her wits. *Come on now, Emily. Get yourself together*, she urged herself.

She waited a beat and decided to make a run for it. She dashed down the corridor and down the stairs running smack into Virginia, whose back was to her.

The girls were stooped over, their silhouettes outlined by two oil lamps that flanked them. As Virginia turned around and Emily's eyes adjusted to the dim light, she sucked in a great breath of horror. Elizabeth was struggling with a human-shaped package.

Emily's brain reeled back, fighting the dawning realization that the package was... *Schlocker's body!*

Elizabeth held onto one dead hand, dragging him, like a discarded bit of furniture, toward the front door. She took a step forward and, feeling something break loose, her load having suddenly lightened, turned around to investigate.

Elizabeth bent over to examine the corpse in the dim light.

Noting that one leg had been left behind, she snatched it up and placed it atop the wrapped bundle.

As she turned back to resume her work, Emily's eyes met hers. A chill smile crept across Elizabeth's mouth. Unable to contain her horror any longer, Emily cried out.

"Schlocker! Oh my god! Schlockerrrr!"

* * *

Elizabeth leapt at the sound. She dropped Schlocker's arm and marched toward Emily, whose scream echoed through the house, even as she stood in place, rendered frozen with fear.

Elizabeth threw her hand up over the screaming O of the woman's mouth, breaking the spell. Emily juked to the side of Elizabeth and ran. As if following a mad woman's map, she ducked in and out of doors, from room to room, the feathered hem of her flimsy night robe held aloft with her darting movements.

The girls giggled, mad with delight as they watched Emily flit room to room to bang on windows. They hid themselves in the shadows, understanding well that their new playmate was not going anywhere, for Bruno had bolted the doors when he left to pick up their shiny, new toy.

Now they had all the time in the world to play hide and seek with Emily!

In a rare show of sisterly solidarity, the girls joined hands to skip-skip about. They separated, each adjourning to a different corner. They huddled low, hiding their giggles behind cupped hands until they could no longer contain their excitement and popped their heads out to call to each other.

"Virginia! I see you!"

"Elizabeth, I see you too!"

Emily had made her way to the parlor, where she cowered near the old desk. She quaked with abject terror. She covered her ears in a desperate attempt to block out the sounds of the girls' taunting footsteps.

"She'll tell on us!" Virginia sang. "She'll *tell, tell, tell.*" The words took on the tune of a child's nursery rhyme.

* * *

As the girls drew closer, Emily's eyes darted about the room, searching for a weapon, a means of escape, anything at all! Having regained at least a bit of her senses, she jumped up and pushed back the desk's roll top. She riffed through the pigeonholes and drawers, tossing aside office supplies and scraps of paper.

Elizabeth and Virginia burst through the doorway, bounding toward Emily, who ran to the only egress in the room — *the window!* In one motion, Emily picked up a side chair and threw it through the window frame, sending a spray of glass out onto the porch.

She climbed over the chair and wriggled herself through the sharp entrance her throw had created. Once she had fallen to the porch, she picked herself up to assess the damage. Her negligee was torn and she had several cuts on her arms and legs, but she looked otherwise remarkably unhurt.

More than that, she was giddy with the excitement of her escape! She ran, wildly veering, uncertain of which way to go in the vast darkness of the yard. As she spun in a circle, her mind racing, she caught the glint of the girl's oil lamp, its light flitting from room to room.

Emily ran toward the driveway, shouting, "Bruno! Bruno! Where are you? You have to stop them!"

As she reached the path that led to the gate, the property's only visible exit, Emily realized that both of the cars were gone. Of course, she thought. Peter had taken her car and now Bruno must have left too. She giggled at the absolute insanity of her situation, but her laugh died off as she spotted the light of the oil lamp at the broken window.

Emily ran once more, casting about the bushes and trees for a hiding spot. As she sprinted toward a row of spiny bushes, her flimsy robe seeming to float in the moonlit wind, she heard the girls' light footsteps and sing-song voices.

Emily ducked down behind a bush, her back pressed into the house, her knees drawn up tightly to her. Elizabeth and Virginia must have set down their lamp. All that Emily could see of them were the moonlit outlines of their bodies.

* * *

Virginia carried her knives, which she clink-clinked together as they searched. The girls took their time with the game, stopping to giggle and peek in impossibly small spaces.

Elizabeth sauntered right by the bush where their prey squatted — so close that Emily had wondered if she couldn't reach out and trip the girl. But the metallic clanging of Virginia's knives warned her from that course of action.

Virginia called out, "Elizabeth, do you see her?"

Elizabeth ducked down, peering into the bushes just to the right of Emily. She thrust a hand into the sticker bush, waving it about. Emily, certain she had been spotted, went limp with relief when the hand disappeared, back into the dark night.

"No. Do you?" Elizabeth asked.

"I think..." Virginia approached Elizabeth, and by proxy, Emily. "I smell a bug."

The girls giggled, a wild, unfettered sound. "Yes," Elizabeth said, teasing. "I do think I smell a bug, now that you mention it!"

"Here, buggy, buggy!" Virginia called, leaning into the bushes.

Her eyes locked on Emily, who jumped up and sprinted toward the backyard. The girls took flight after her, flanking on either side. Emily was caught into the open yard, spinning in circles. "Here, bug! Come here little bug!" Virginia sang.

* * *

As the woman turned, the images blending, a horrible tableau of the two girls and the skeletal trees and the house, with its turrets and eyes for windows —

With nowhere else to go, Emily bolted away from the girls and toward the fence that encircled the back of the property. She tripped on the hem of her robe and spilled forward. She collected herself and stood up, finding herself face to face with —

Ralph! He caught her, his arms wrapped tightly around her, a bear hug. The girls ran toward them, a wild inertia driving a zigzagging path toward their prey. Ralph lifted Emily off the ground, jumping with excitement. He'd caught her and his sisters would be proud of him!

"Ralphie, Ralphie, Ralphie!" Virginia exclaimed as they closed in on their hapless victim.

Ralph grinned at Virginia and wrapped his arms even more tightly, crushing Emily to him. The woman had given up all pretense of dignity. Her robe hung in long dangly ribbons of ripped gauze and fur. Sticks and bits of dried leaves littered her hair, her face smeared with tears and dirt.

Emily sucked in at the cool air, but she could smell nothing but Ralph's sour breath and the rank odor of his yellowed undershirt. She attempted to calm herself, muttering under her breath an exercise a therapist had taught her many years before.

Of course, that was the same day that she called said therapist a quack before marching out of his office in a huff.

As she hung there, limp in Ralph's arms, repeating the mantra "Just breathe. Breathe in. Hold. Breathe out," over and over, she was inclined to believe she had been right.

The breathing exercise did nothing but highlight the

predicament she was in, for as Ralph hugged tighter to his sister's squeals and cheers, she was increasingly aware of her waning breath. Her ribs seemed like an iron cage, pushing in on her soft, pink lungs. She tilted her head backward, sucking at the night air above her, wheezing.

Ralph squeezed tighter still. She felt her last lungful of air exit; no matter how she concentrated, pulling her chest muscles inward in an attempt to force oxygen in, nothing would come. She gasped, a fish out of water. The edges of her vision went first gray, then black, until the entire frame of her eyes was darkness. Emily's limp body slipped from Ralph's embrace.

Ralph covered his ears and looked from one sister to another. His lip quivered with uncertainty, twisting in an attempt to make himself heard. "I… do… bad…?"

Elizabeth put a protective arm around him. "No, Ralphie. She was bad."

Virginia dropped to her knees and climbed astride Emily's prone body. She lifted her knives high in the air above the woman's neck, proclaiming, "I caught a big fat bug in my web!"

Chapter Twenty-Two

Peter steered Emily's sports car down a city street, with a slightly-wobbly-from-alcohol Anne at his side. He drove just as one might expect a man to, when he was likely just over the legal limit for alcohol to drive: under the speed limit with the occasional quick jerk to bring the wheels back into his lane.

He pulled up to the front office of a quaint roadside motel. Peter and Anne peered out the window; they saw the neon sign beside the office. "No Vacancy."

Peter slapped the steering wheel. "Dangit, Anne. I'm so sorry. That's the last one."

Anne sighed. "I guess we shouldn't have spine all that time at the — uh — what was that place called?" She rubbed her forehead, as if calling forth the answer. "Village Inn."

"You're right. I didn't realize how late it was getting. You lose count when they keep taking the glasses away like that!"

"Oh, not me! I know exactly how many..." Anne began to count on her fingers, holding them up one by one. She loses track when she reaches four, putting them all down to restart the count.

"Well, the next town is fifty miles. I'm afraid there's nothing to do but double up with Schlocker and Emily back at the house. Ugh. He probably snores, too."

Anne giggled. "Yes, he does. Terribly!" Peter did a good old-fashioned double take that prompted Anne to add, "Every afternoon, with his feet propped up on the desk and his head back like..." Anne threw her head back and let out an ear-shattering snorting sound.

Peter giggled, which set Anne to giggling. They faced each other, their giggles growing to howling laughter. Anne struggled to catch her breath.

"You are so funny!" she cried. "You thought..."

"Oh, no. I would never think that!"

"Schlocker..." Anne held her finger up under her nose, an imitation of his bushy mustache.

"Schlocker!" Peter howled.

The two of them sat there for a moment, their giggle fit slowing until all that remained was an awkward silence.

"Well, I guess we had better be getting back to the house then, hadn't we..." Peter ventured.

Anne nodded in agreement. Peter started the car and headed back down the road they had come from. He was clearly having trouble keeping the car on the straight and narrow and Anne could sense his annoyance. "You'll have to forgive my being so silly! Martinis always do this to me, Mr... pardon me." Anne stifled a hiccup. "Mr... what was your name again?"

"It's alright. And it's Peter, to you."

"Oh. Then, how do you do Mr. Peter-to-you? I think I like that much better than Howe, you know. Think how silly it would sound if I ever married anybody with a name like that. Anne Howe!"

"Good lord, you're right. I hadn't thought of that. We'd better turn back, before it's too late."

"Turn back? Why is it already too late, don't you think..."

Anne searched his face, trying to understand him. He turned his head toward her, the car veering slightly off its path. It lurched forward, the wheels grinding against the gravel of the shoulder as an oncoming car barreled past them, blaring its horn!

* * *

Bruno pounded on the horn one more time for good measure. He never could understand people driving that way, and with the current state of his nerves, he was in no condition to withstand such a shock. Why that car had nearly hit him, head on!

He reached up to wipe the tears from his cheek. They flowed freely, an endless stream rolling down onto his collar. It was cold comfort, the knowledge that he held deep in his heart, that he was doing the right thing.

I promised I would take care of them… no matter what.

Chapter Twenty-Three

Ralph slept soundly, curled up like a cat atop the sideboard that held the good china, with his thumb resting comfortably in his blood-speckled mouth. Virginia turned her head to look at him, with a smile of contentment she turned back to the project at hand.

The girls had spread out hundreds of jigsaw puzzle pieces across the table. There was no photo or box to guide them and they did not seem to have made any progress. Elizabeth picked up two pieces, seemingly at random, twisting at the edges in an attempt to get them to fit. When she could not make them mesh, she held up an offending piece up and tore off its corner then tossed it aside. She picked up another piece and jammed it forcibly onto a random piece, laying the two mismatched bits out on the table with a triumphant smile.

"See," Elizabeth said. "I told you I could do it!"

Virginia rolled her eyes at her sister's simplicity. She picked up the joined pieces, flinging them to the far edges of the table.

"That will take foreeeeeeever. Do it like this..." Virginia insisted.

Elizabeth turned her head away, her cheeks burning, bright crimson. Virginia frowned. She stared her sister down, willing her to look. Virginia poked her sister, hard, in the arm but Elizabeth only crossed her arms in defiance.

"You do it like this," Virginia muttered.

She speared one of the puzzle pieces with one of her serrated knives, darting the piece onto another, then another, before stabbing the entire stack onto the table top. Quite content with her game of darts, she paused only when she caught a flicker of movement in the corner of her eye.

A spider, small and black, crawled from beneath a splayed book, traversing the maze of puzzle pieces. Virginia watched with interest, her knife poised just above it. Her eyes traced its tracks, but she did not strike. Instead, she dropped the knife and with a shocking suddenness, snatched up the spider with a practiced stroke.

She held it in her hand for a moment, waving her closed fist in front of her sister who only stuck out her tongue and said, "Ew."

Virginia popped the spider into her mouth. She was always delighted in watching her sister's sickened expression and tonight was no different.

Elizabeth gagged. "EW! Spiders aren't supposed to eat other spiders, you know."

Virginia shrugged. She crouched down, a spider leg popping from between her lips. She promptly sucked it back into her mouth. "Cannibal spiders do!"

Both girls turned their heads, forgetting their spat. They ran toward the sound of Bruno's approaching car, watching through the window for his lights to appear. Virginia promptly forgot all worries of being in trouble, so great was her joy at Bruno's belated arrival.

She clapped, running to the front door, shouting. "Bruno! Bruno!"

Elizabeth frowned. "That doesn't sound like Bruno's car," she said.

Virginia pressed her face into the dirty glass and squinted

into the darkness. "Oh no! It's Uncle Peter and the pretty lady! Why did they come back?"

Elizabeth joined her sister at the window. "Now, Virginia. Bruno said I was in charge, so you have to listen to me! You mustn't play spider with anyone else tonight. Or else Bruno will really hate you!"

"He will not," Virginia replied. "Anyway, I like Uncle Peter. I think he's nice. Not like that bad man!"

"All the same. They might tell on us and then we'll be in big trouble!"

Virginia's face dropped. "Would they? Would they really tell? I don't think that Uncle Peter would do that. But I don't know about the pretty lady…"

"Of course, they'll tell!" Elizabeth hissed. "Bruno said there would be other bad people, didn't he?"

The car lurched to a halt outside.

"They're coming!" Virginia cried. "What do we do?!"

Elizabeth's face lit up. "We'll have to make a plan!"

* * *

Outside, Peter set the emergency brake. He fumbled with the key, heaving a sigh of relief as the car engine grumbled to sleep. He glanced into his rearview mirror.

"Are you all right, Peter?" Anne asked.

"Oh… I'm fine but… I must be smashed. I could have sworn I saw… I mean, it must have been that patch of moonlight back there shining on something in the yard. I could have sworn it looked like Emily."

Anne stifled a giggle. They truly were smashed! "Do you like to see things in the clouds?" she asked, her head lolling back into the seat rest, eyes half-closing.

Ignoring her question, Peter said, "Well, it looks like there is still somebody up and about. See the light?" He pointed to the window.

Anne pulled herself out of her stupor. Her stomach was roiling and, although she would have much preferred to stay at the inn, she had resolved herself to be happy with a warm bed and a pillow.

"I hope it's not that Ralph," Anne said.

"Aww, Ralph's all right. He's just a big…"

"A big kid. I know. You said that, but he's … well, he's…" Anne lowered her voice, hesitating before adding, "Really big!"

Peter could not help but chuckle at her earnest reply and big-as-saucers eyes. "Oh, Anne. He's harmless as a baby!"

Anne let out another belch. She covered her mouth, embarrassed. "Do you really think so?"

Peter laid a steadying hand atop Anne's. Even as drunk as he was, with his thoughts swimming and his body feeling as floaty as if he'd set off in a hot air balloon — even with all this, his feelings toward this woman who sat beside him were making themselves clear.

Anne looked down at their hands, stacked as they were, and smiled.

"Everything will be fine," Peter assured her. By way of proving it, he exited the car, tripping only once on the way to Anne's side.

He opened her door, offering her an elbow — which was a good thing, as Anne's high-heeled gait was even more wonky than Peter's. Locked together, they traversed the shadowy path that led to the house.

Peter paused, tilting his head upward to observe the skies. "Well, I'll be, Anne." Peter pointed a shaky finger upward.

"Hmm," Anne said. "I hadn't noticed before. It's a full moon."

Peter nodded. He could not help but think that it did seem somehow fitting. As they resumed their approach, the front door opened, revealing Elizabeth and Virginia.

The girls had cleaned up. They no longer wore pajamas, but yet another in their seemingly endless collection of anachronistic dresses, loose, shapeless, the type of dress designed for little girls, with frilly lace trims around the hems and the sleeves.

The girls smiled sweetly, Virginia dropping into one of the exaggerated curtsies she so favored. Elizabeth whispered to her sister through gritted teeth. "What are they doing here?"

Virginia merely elbowed her by way of reply. Her voice rang out, saccharine sweet. "Good evening, Uncle Peter!" she shouted.

Peter helped Anne along toward the steps. Anne stopped in front of them, a look of uncertainty crossing her face. She held tight to Peter's arm as she removed her patent leather pumps, tossing them unceremoniously to the side. Peter chuckled and grabbed hold of her elbow again. It was less the show of chivalry that he hoped it played as than a concern that if he let go of her they'd both tumble right to the ground.

Elizabeth muttered under her breath. "I think they are drunk skunks."

"Mmhmm," Virginia replied.

Face to face with the girls, Peter smiled warmly. "Hi, Kids! I'm afraid Miss Morse and I will have to stay the night here after all. No room at the inn as they say!"

Virginia smiled her uncanny smile — the smile which, only a few hours previous, Peter had written off as the awkward greeting of a sweet, if confused, little girl. But now, the smile unnerved him. There was something *off* about it.

Still, she is just a child, he thought, and did his best to shake off that feeling of unease.

Anne squeezed Peter's hand tightly, pumping it a few times. He took it as a sign that she too was feeling uncomfortable and took it as a cue to inquire about the others.

"Say, girls. Ahh — where is Mr. Bruno? Is he around?" he asked, as he peeked around the girls into the dark house beyond.

Elizabeth shifted her weight, moving the block Peter's view.

It was more for the sport than to hide anything, for Emily's body laid in the yard, in plain view of the car. Further, the interior of the house lay shrouded in the late night darkness.

"No," Virginia replied. "Bruno is away right now."

"This late? Hmm," Peter said.

"Oh, he'll be back soon," Elizabeth said.

Virginia pushed the door open. "Do come in."

Peter and Anne approached the door with overly cautious steps. As they stepped over the threshold, a frown crossed Peter's face. A realization. "Girls, ah – your Aunt Emily? Is she…" He motioned his arms at their surroundings.

The sisters ushered Anne and Peter inside. Virginia spun on her heel and made haste to slam the door shut, locking the door's multiple latches and knobs.

"Elizabeth, dear," Peter said. He had decided to try a different tack with the girls, lowering his voice to a gentle croon. "We're so grateful for your hospitality. But I would like to wish my sister goodnight. Do you know if she has — ah —" His pickled brain struggled to produce the word he sought. "Ah… has she — retired?"

Elizabeth approached her uncle and, under Anne's wary stare, lifted a single pointer figure and rested it on his lips.

"*Shhhhhh,*" she intoned. Virginia joined in with her sister, the two of them hissing like angered snakes.

Peter shook his head in confusion, lifting his hand to gently move Elizabeth's finger away from his face. She snatched her hand back and pointed at the ceiling.

"Oh," Anne said. "She must be asleep, Peter."

Anne smiled through gritted teeth. Her eyes darted back and forth, from the doorways that circled the room to the girl's faces and back. She did not know what she was looking for, only that she felt the cold grip of fear tugging at her, insistent.

She desperately wanted to leave but no amount of squeezing and pulling at Peter's hand seemed to get that point across. Instead, he turned to her and shot her a dazzlingly perfect smile. It was enough to convince her that she was alone in her concerns.

Virginia raised her finger to her own lips and eased in closer to Anne, such that her face hovered mere inches from her.

"*Shhhhhhhhh!*" she said again.

Peter's discomfort had given way to drunken amusement at the strange situation. He, too, raised a finger, copying them with a loud, "*Shhhhhh!*"

Anne did not find any of this funny, but she had no option but to stand there, awkwardly shifting as she waited for the moment to end.

Elizabeth took up the oil lamp from a nearby table and motioned for Peter and Anne to follow them into the adjoining drawing room. Neither of them noticed the shattered window behind them.

"We should sit and wait for Bruno," Elizabeth said. She'd lowered her voice, back to its formerly calm and sweet timber. "There isn't any need to disturb anyone."

"Of course!" Peter replied, a bit too loudly, his sense of volume control having left him two martinis before. "So, ah, how soon will Mr. Bruno be —"

Elizabeth cut him off. "Oh, he'll be along soon. Don't worry! You should make yourself right at home. Virginia, you may entertain Uncle Peter while I take care of the pretty lady." Elizabeth flashed a toothy grin at Anne.

"Oh," Anne said. "Oh, I'm fine. I —"

Peter jumped in. "Anne, go on! I'm sure Elizabeth knows what to do."

Elizabeth had already corralled the woman to the side, away from Peter, and slipped her elbow into Anne's.

"Well," Anne said, mostly to Peter. "If you really think so..."

"Yes, yes. You should get some rest. Elizabeth can take you to Emily's room. And I wouldn't worry. Emily isn't all that bad to get along with. At least not when she's asleep." Peter let out a snort of appreciation for his own joke. Anne was not amused.

Elizabeth pulled Anne toward the stairs. "Oh, that won't be necessary! We can put Anne in my daddy's room. He won't mind. It's very nice in there"

Anne shook her head, confused. Her father, she thought. Bruno had mentioned his death, hadn't he? Wasn't that the entire reason they were here, to check on the inheritance?! What was she talking about?

She noted Peter's seeming ease which, in turn, quelled her worries, at least insofar as the room was concerned. Certainly the girls must have meant that she could sleep in their late father's room... though, if she thought about that too long, it would have given her the willies. Anne was not much for ghosts.

"Why does that sound great, doesn't it? No roommates for you! Meanwhile, I'll be stuck with Schlocker's snoring," Peter said.

"Yes," Anne replied to Elizabeth. "That would be nice. You're very kind." Anne moved toward Peter. "Good night, Peter."

"I'll see you in the morning, Miss — Anne," Peter stood there, hands in his pockets, school-boy-shuffling.

Spontaneously, as if drawn together by an outside force, their hands met. Anne took Peter's hand — oh that liquid courage, for she was not under ordinary circumstances the kind of girl who would take such initiative — and lifted it gently to her lips. She kissed his fingertips. Her face flushed red with the sugar high of love.

"It's been awfully nice," she said as Elizabeth grabbed her other hand, breaking the two of them apart. The girl half-dragged, half-led Anne toward the stairs.

Peter muttered to himself, turning his hand over before he dropped it to his side. "Wow."

"This way, pretty lady," Elizabeth cooed, leading the way up the stairs.

Anne, despite her dizziness, upped the pace so that

Elizabeth would let her hand go. She held onto the rail for dear life, remembering for the first time since they'd entered the house, that she had left her shoes outside.

Oh well, she thought. *Too late for that now!*

"See you in the morning, Miss Morse!" Peter called out enthusiastically as he watched Elizabeth and Anne disappear into the upstairs hallway.

Now that Virginia was alone with Peter the curiosity that had been eating at her took its full hold. She cocked her head at him, studying his face.

"I'm glad you came back, Uncle Peter. I like you."

"Why, thank you," Peter slurred. "I like you too, Virginia."

Peter sways, his eyes fluttering. Truth be told, he knew he had overdone it, but the excitement of talking with Anne had tempered the effects of the alcohol or at least provided distraction from them. But now, his head pounded, his tongue went thick and dry.

"You like me?" Virginia asked. She batted her lashes at him. To anyone who had consumed less liquor than Peter had it was an obvious, if amateurish, imitation of adult flirting. But Peter merely giggled and rubbed his aching temples.

Chapter Twenty-Four

Elizabeth led Anne down the corridor, cooing and pointing out different features of the house along the way. She lifted her oil lamp to throw a yellow glow over the taxidermied condor with its gore-drenched beak.

Anne nodded politely, fighting back nausea as the girl detailed the day that her and her father had come across the dead condor. "He must have been hit by a car, maybe, while he was eating that mouse. It was sad. So Daddy said that we could bring him home and stuff him!"

Anne managed a half-smile, which greatly pleased and encouraged Elizabeth.

"You're a nice lady. You're not like those others! I liked you right away. Virginia told me that she likes you too. And Ralph! We all like you, pretty lady."

Elizabeth leaned in close to Anne, whispering into her ear. "I think Peter likes you, too."

Anne pulled back from Elizabeth, who had paused before a bedroom door. She swung it open, wide enough to allow Anne to enter ahead of her. Elizabeth backed into the room ahead of Anne, carefully placing herself between the guest and the bed.

All at once, Elizabeth's demeanor changed. Her smile fell

back into a straight line. She stood up straight, authoritative, one hand poised, stiff, on her hip. The timber of her voice dropped, the saccharine sweetness gone. "You would never tell on us. I know you wouldn't, no matter what Bruno says!"

Elizabeth took one step to the side then, revealing the bed. Anne stood there, a few feet from the bed, in silence. It took her a few minutes for her brain to register what she was seeing, for she had no context for the horror that lay in that bed.

She considered each possible scenario. *Maybe it was the alcohol? Can alcohol cause you to see things? No, maybe not, but it could affect vision and judgment, couldn't it? Perhaps this is all a gag, some kind of prank? She thought, though she quickly dismissed that idea. What else was there?*

When the only possibility left was that yes, indeed, there was a rotting corpse tucked into the bed, she backed away, slowly.

As she turned to flee the room, Ralph popped out at her from his hiding spot behind the door. He clapped his hands over her mouth and spun her around so that she was caught in his bear hug. Anne kicked her bare feet, twisting herself up and down in Ralph's iron grasp.

"Ralphie, be careful!" Elizabeth admonished him. "You would never tell! I know you wouldn't! And Ralph knows you wouldn't too. I like you pretty lady."

Ralph ran his greasy fingers through Anne's curls.

Chapter Twenty-Five

Bruno was barely recognizable, having given up his customary livery for a faded work shirt and pants. The look on his face lay somewhere between sadness and relief. *You always knew it would come to this.*

He parked the Dusseldorf off on the shoulder at the bottom of the pile of rubble that surrounded the blasting site. Armed only with a flashlight and a large leather satchel, he picked his way over the rocky terrain. He managed the best he could; it was difficult to navigate in the darkness. More than once, he tripped over the errant rock or bit of debris. His knees ached something horrible. But sheer dogged determination won the day, and he marched onward.

By the time he reached his destination, he had sweated clean through his shirt and his silvery hair hung in limp strands. He stopped to gather his breath, having reached his destination — an olive drab prefab shed festooned with several hand-painted signs that read DANGER and KEEP OUT. He chuckled to himself, thinking how the danger signs had brought him to the right place.

Bruno fished a crowbar from his satchel and set to work on the bright red padlock that guarded the door. He pushed the crowbar's tip into the lock assembly, bracing himself against the shed for leverage. Bruno huffed and puffed, wrenching the bar back and forth until, at last, the padlock snapped open, letting loose of its rusted-out chain.

He dropped the padlock and leaned into the shed, struggling to even out his breaths, embarrassed — though there was no one to see — at how out of shape and silly he must have appeared in that moment, like some kind of past his prime cat burglar.

But there was no time to waste, so he set back to work once he'd caught his breath. He pulled the chain free and threw the shed doors open wide to the moonlight.

Chapter Twenty-Six

Peter was doing his level best to be a good sport, but between his sour stomach, which roiled and begged for a cracker to settle it, and the binding that Virginia was wrapping ever more tightly around him, his patience for the game was waning fast.

Virginia circled the high-backed rocking chair he sat in, wrapping layer after layer of lacy fabric about him. Peter bucked forward and realized, suddenly, that he could not move at all.

What if Virginia tires of this game? Why, if she walked away, I'd be trapped in this cocoon all night.

"Virginia," Peter did his very best to keep his voice lightly conversational despite the strange circumstances. "I'm getting a bit tired. It's been fun playing *Spider* with you, but I think I'd best be off to bed soon."

Virginia continued to circle without pause. She hummed her tuneless little song, dancing about him on her tiptoes without so much as an acknowledgment that he had spoken at all. She stopped and approached him, leaning in close to place a hand on Peter's cheek. "Uncle Peter, you must be quiet so I can finish the game!"

Peter smiled uncomfortably and settled back into the chair, hoping that she would finish whatever the last part of the game entailed, and soon! Not only was his stomach gurgling, the alcohol had found its way to his bladder and he wasn't sure how much longer he would last in that chair.

Virginia backed up and spread her arms, a grand dramatic sweep. "And then the big black spider goes round and round and round and wraps the bug all up in her spiderweb! Just like you!"

Peter did not like the look on Virginia's face. Although he would not have been able to explain it, something in her had shifted somehow. It was her eyes, he thought. There was a sudden storminess about them.

"Virginia, what happens in this game when the spider gets the bug all wrapped up?"

Virginia rested her fingertips on Peter's lips. "Ahaaa! I'll never tell!"

"Oh, I understand. It's a secret. But how long does it take to play this game?"

Virginia smiled and pulled back into a dainty innocent-little-girl stance, her hands folded neatly in front of her waist. "We're almost done!" Virginia circled the chair and gave it a playful pull backwards. It wobbled, nearly tipping over, to Peter's obvious discomfort.

"There now! Little Bug!" She moved around to face her uncle once more, as if to contemplate the handiwork, but caught a hint of movement behind the chair.

Virginia watched as the dumbwaiter slowly descended into its shaft from the rooms above, revealing two pairs of feet, then the rest of the bodies. Ralph was doubled up, squished into half of the dumbwaiter in a sort of upright fetal position with Anne on her knees beside him. They were wedged in tight, their heads ducked at strange angles. Ralph's hand was clapped over Anne's mouth.

Virginia gave Ralph a little wave as the dumbwaiter

continued on its downward track, taking Ralph and Anne once more out of view. Peter's voice tore her away from her spying.

"All right, Virginia. What does the spider do now?" he asked, impatient.

"What?" she asked, shaking her head as if to remember where they had been moments before. "Oh, yes! Umm, now the spider does a little dance for the bug."

Virginia wiggled her arms, long languorous movements that are more like a snake bundling itself around its prey than a spider.

Peter cleared his throat and did his best to avert his eyes while pretending to watch. Virginia's dance was both disturbingly seductive and childlike all at once.

"Say, Virginia. I think we'd better finish up this game —"

Virginia cut him off, dancing closer to him. "Uncle Peter, do you like that pretty lady?"

"Why yes, I do." He hoped against hope that this was the answer that Virginia was angling for.

"Do you like me?"

"Yes, Virginia, of course I do. But..."

Virginia danced closer, closer. She quivered, excited at the nearness.

A cold sweat broke across his forehead. "Uh, Virginia – when do you think Mr. Bruno will be back?"

"It's all right," she replied. "Bruno won't hate me. He told me that he won't hate me no matter what!"

Virginia caressed Peter's face as she rocked the chair to and fro. "Spiders like bugs!" she crooned. Virginia's teeth found Peter's throat and she nipped him. He froze. "Bugs taste good!"

Peter turned his head to the side, the best he could do to escape her.

"But I guess that bugs don't like spiders very much," Virginia said. She drew back to contemplate Peter, disappointed at his lack of response.

Peter's reply came as a hoarse gasp. "Oh, I do like spiders. It's just…"

His words were lost as Virginia jumped up and beelined for the roll top desk.

"I do too," she said. "But I guess I have to sting you now!" Virginia peeled back to the desktop with an alarmingly loud *thunk*.

Peter watched her dig through the desk, her back to him, the cold sweat pooling at his collar. He tensed his muscles, hoping to find enough space to work an arm free. It was no use. The binding was too tight for that.

Virginia swiveled around to face her uncle. She wielded her two knives, crossed before her chest. She sliced them back and forth, the edges clinking together as she marched toward Peter. Unable to reason or deny away the danger he was in anymore, the cold sweat of fear crashed through Peter's drunkenness, rendering him suddenly sober.

Peter's voice rose — he could only hope that someone else in the house would hear him, but he didn't think it wise to call for help, not with Virginia standing just a few feet from him, her knives poised to strike!

"Ah, Virginia. Is Mr. Schlocker here? Mr. Schlocker? Are you here?"

Virginia rushed forward, a whirlwind, advancing with the knives thrust outward at her jaws, giving the appearance of a spider's falces! Peter flinched, eyes shut tight, bracing for the impact!

"Sting! Sting!" Virginia sang, then — suddenly — stopped, mere inches from Peter's throat. Virginia withdrew and turned toward the dining room, where Elizabeth beckoned her with desperate hand movements.

Virginia glanced at Peter, at her sister, and back again. "Uncle Peter, I have to go away for just a minute. But I will be right back!"

Peter, unsure of how to react, could only nod.

"Don't go away, Bug!" she sang as she skipped to join her sister.

Peter's face was a mask of absolute blood-curdled terror, his voice choked off in retches. He watched as Virginia rushed to the doorway to join her sister and the two of them skipped off to the cellar stairs, toward the sound of Anne's muffled cries.

Chapter Twenty-Seven

Ralph and Anne were tangled, a pile of limbs, at the bottom of the cellar stairs. He struggled to hold Anne firm against him but it was like grabbing a tiger by the tail.

Anne struggled with a violence so unexpected that Virginia couldn't help but be impressed. Ralph managed to keep one hand over her mouth through all the scuffling such that Anne's cries were more of a kitten mewing than a tiger.

The girls watched with interest but neither made any move towards them. Elizabeth turned to her sister. "What are we going to do with her? Ralph can't let her go now. She'll tell!"

"What do you mean, what are we going to do? Don't you know? You are supposed to be in charge. Didn't Bruno say that?"

Elizabeth looked as if she might burst out crying. "Bruno will be so angry at me. I don't know what to do." She was entirely deflated.

Virginia waved her sister away. It wasn't like her to be such a big baby, Virginia thought, empathy being entirely beyond her. She moved down a few steps. Anne's eyes lit up as they caught hers, hoping that the girl might help her. But Virginia merely watched with a dark interest.

"She wiggles, doesn't she? Just like a big, squiggly-wiggly bug in a spiderweb!"

Ralph raised his eyebrows and shrugged, wailing at his sister for help. Virginia waved to Elizabeth and the two of them approached, with Virginia in the lead. She felt quite proud in that moment, knowing that Bruno had appointed Elizabeth as the head of the siblings in his absence, yet here *she* was — all grown up — leading her sister along.

Virginia stood very close to Ralph and Anne now. She cocked her head, examining them. Anne had gone limp in Ralph's arms, though Virginia knew she was not dead by the snorting sound of her uneven breaths.

Behind Ralph and Anne, the out of sight pit dwellers moaned and scuffled about, sensing the presence of flesh not far from the reach of their clawed hands and endlessly hungry mouths.

All at once, Anne took up her struggle, knocking Ralph a hard upward shot to the chin.

Ralph moved to muffle her piercing shriek, while pitifully rubbing his injured jaw with his free hand.

"Uncle Ned could make her quiet!" Elizabeth said.

"No," Virginia replied. "Bruno would be very mad. Anyway, Ralph likes her, see? We mustn't hurt her. Just make her quiet!"

It was easier said than done, the problem an obvious challenge in logic. But Virginia considered herself very much up for solving this puzzle, having now anointed herself their de facto leader. Her brows knitted with effort. "Well… now, a spider is very clever. She very cleverly drains the vital juice from the bug's body. And that makes the bug stop squiggling!"

Virginia raised her finger in imitation of the scientists she had seen in movies. *Eureka*, she thought. She was not sure what it meant, but it sounded like an official, science-like word.

"Would that make her stop squiggling?" Elizabeth asked and Virginia nodded in the affirmative. "Then I think we should do it!"

Virginia nodded again. She made a beeline for the row of gardening tools that lined the wall near the coffins that had proved Schlocker's undoing. Her fingers glided over the handles of various implements. "I have to find something very sharp!" she declared.

Anne redoubled her violent efforts to escape Ralph's grip. Anne reeled back, letting her body fall nearly limp, creating a space between her and Ralph. She used that bit of space to wind up, pulling her leg back and kicking Ralph so hard that he flew backwards, landing against the precariously propped coffin, which wobbled and fell forward, knocking Virginia off-balance.

* * *

Upstairs, Peter heard Anne's muffled cries and fought against his binding with renewed effort. The rocking chair slid and shook with his efforts to inch the rocking chair forward. It occurred to him that he had no particular plan to escape. He could hurl himself from the window, he supposed. But then wouldn't he be stuck — possibly face down — on the porch? And still tied to the rocking chair. No, that didn't seem like a plan.

He searched the room as best he could from his position, circling his head to one side then the other. As he slowly inched the rocker in a circle, he spotted his salvation. There, on the roll top desk, lay Virginia's knives!

He rocked and jerked, inching his way ever closer, hoping that Virginia would stay otherwise occupied long enough ...

Chapter Twenty-Eight

The moonlight breeze danced, ghost-like, among the skeletal boughs that flanked the porch of Merrye House. In a patch of blue light, Emily lay motionless atop a bed of compost and fungi. Her glittering eyes were open now, staring at the full moon above.

An owl hooted, a beckoning shibboleth, and Emily twitched, lips parting into a leer. She rose from the bed, stiff, ghostlike. Her movements were those of a soul freed from the grave. An otherworldly sound, a moan, escaped her, morphing into a single word stretched out over many syllables.

"Ralph… Raaaaaalph…"

Emily, now upright, lurched through the weed-jungle of the yard, her ragged lacy gown undulating through shadows and moonlight as she searched, calling out over and over. *Raaaalph. Ralllllllllllllph.*

* * *

Elizabeth had joined Ralph in his struggle to hold Anne still, having wrestled her body up onto the long ceramic drainboard next to the sink. Virginia was poised above her, a hacksaw in one hand, her other pressing down on Anne's calf in a desperate attempt to still the clawing figure.

Anne turned her shoulder to ward off the blows of Anne's other leg as it threshed wildly about. Ralph's cupped hand over her mouth did little to mute her piercing screams of terror. Elizabeth, who had been standing by, jumped in to help restrain Anne, wrapping her arms around the woman's kicking legs.

With Anne firmly in place, Virginia could finally get to work. "Hold her still," she declared. "I just have to make a little teeny cut."

Elizabeth looked up at Virginia, who had grabbed hold of Anne's ankle. "Virginia, how much should we let run out?" It was a question rooted in genuine curiosity.

Virginia paused, her forehead furrowing in deep thought. "Just enough until she gets quiet. Then Ralph can hold her better." Ralph jumped up and down with excitement at the mention of his name; it was the only word that registered any meaning for him at all.

Anne twisted and kicked with renewed energy. Anne's foot caught Virginia in the chest, sending her backward and once more into another of the coffins, which topped over. As that one fell, it sent the others wobbling and one by one, crashing to the floor. Several of them split open from the impact, spilling their contents — mushy, half-mummified remains, much of it now crushed to bits — onto the floor. The bones that roll into the pit behind them are met with cries of surprised excitement.

* * *

Peter stopped long enough to catch his breath. It was much harder work than it would seem, as evidenced by his red, sweat-drenched face. His eyelids fluttered, the alcohol lulling him into a trance that was swiftly interrupted by the sound of the crashing coffins below.

Peter took up his efforts once more, rotating the rocking

chair a few inches with each thrust of his body. He inched closer, closer until his clutching fingers skimmed the knife blades. Still, try as he might, he could not quite grab hold of them.

"*Ralphiiiiiie...*" Emily's thin voice rang in the air behind Peter.

He spun his head to the right but could not see anything beyond the front window. Still, he was elated — he'd know that voice anywhere! He called out to his sister who, unfortunately and unbeknownst to him, continued down the hallway in that stilted way, searching for Ralph.

"No, not that way, Emily! In here! Emily! Help!" Peter twisted his head again, as far as he could but couldn't catch more than the edge of the doorway which Emily had just passed.

"Oh no! Emily! Come on... I'm in here!" he cried, his voice taking on an imploring, desperate tone. "Emily, where have you been? For heaven's sake, will you come give me a hand. I'm tied up. That little fiend got me all..." Peter's words died off with the sense that he was being watched.

Emily appeared in the doorway behind him. Her eyes, while fixated on Peter, seemed to stare straight through him. She resumed her ghostly walk toward the dining room, leaving her brother in near-tears. At the head of the stairs, she paused, listening, haloed in the light from beyond.

* * *

Ralph was growing tired but, not wanting to disappoint his sister, he did his best to hold the pretty lady down. All of these were vague thoughts of course, more simple caveman-like pictures and feelings, flooding the maze of his remaining neurons.

Anne's legs continued to twist and thrash, if more slowly. She was clearly running out of steam.

Virginia took the opportunity to grab onto Anne's ankles, forcing them together under one hand, the other wielding the rusty hacksaw. She lifted the saw high, above her head, then lowered it slowly, stopping just before the blade touched Anne's skin, delighting in the terror-filled screams. Virginia lined the hacksaw up, wondering, was it better to cut at the knee or further down? Hmm. She tilted her head, lost in thought, the hacksaw still poised but a foot above Anne's quivering legs. "I wish you would just hold still, pretty lady!" she cried in frustration.

She raised the saw again, and Emily flinched, shutting her eyes tight, certain that this would be the final blow. Something in Virginia's expression has shifted. There was a sort of determination that hadn't been present before.

The tip of Virginia's tongue peeked through the corner of her lips, a mark of concentration. As she raised the saw once more, a shadow fell over Anne's figure, interrupting her work.

"Oh, darn it!" she yelled. Her concentration destroyed, she turned toward the source of disruption.

Emily floated toward them, her ghostly figure casting a long shadow. The thing that had been Emily — who, it would seem, was no more — pivoted its head toward the source of its search, Ralph. She let out a cry, and inhuman shriek and — all at once — rushed toward Ralph.

His eyes went wide as she fell upon him, tackling him to the floor. They tumbled amid the broken coffin debris, their bodies rolling and crushing the bits of bone and dry skin that littered the ground. It was not clear, perhaps not even to the thing that once was Emily, whether the attack was born of lust or anger, or both, for her hands found Ralph's throat.

Emily caressed the hollow of his collarbones with dirt-stained fingertips, then closed those same hands around his neck while he cried out in anguish, gurgling and choking. Emily cackled, her small hands surprisingly strong, closing in on Ralph.

Behind them, the pit stirred with activity. The melee above had excited the pit-dwellers,

attuned as they were to not only the smell of blood, but cries of anguish. They added their inhuman groans to the cacophony of sound.

Virginia and Elizabeth, stunned, dropped their hands and backed away in silent horror. Ralph clawed at his neck, his upturned eyes focused on Virginia. He reached for her, his fingernails grazing her calf.

The touch of Ralph's cold fingers broke Virginia's stupor and she jumped atop Emily's back, prying desperately at the fingers that encircled Ralph's neck.

Anne seized the opportunity to pull herself upright on the drainboard, ripping the seam of her pencil skirt all the way up the side so that she could easily swing her legs off the side. Elizabeth swiftly pushed her back, pinning her once more to the cold metal slab.

Anne gathered what little breath she had left in her and screamed. "Peter, help me!"

Although her instinct was to bolt straight up and run for the hills, she quickly realized her battered body would have none of it. Elizabeth, who had turned her focus to Ralph's terrifying predicament, clapped a hand over her mouth to quiet her. Anne nipped and gnashed at the invading hand while —

On the floor, Emily fastened her hands at Ralph's temples, digging her fingertips into his eye sockets. Virginia kicked at Emily's legs.. She cheered Ralph on, offering enthusiastic boos and screeches.

"Get her Ralph!" she shouted, even as it became clearer still that Ralph's part in the altercation had shifted to that of a helpless victim.

Ralph reached a clawing hand out toward his sister, moaning garbled syllables through the veil of blood that covered his visage.

* * *

"Peter, help!'

Anne's cries heartened Peter, who had gone nearly catatonic from the exhaustion of rocking the chair all the way across the room. But now he was within reach of the knives. They taunted him from the roll-top desk, as he stretched his arms wide, his fingertips just grazing the handle. He grunted with the effort, twisting his trunk to flip his arm just so.

"Hold on, Anne! I'm coming! I'm on the way!"

Peter launched his Plan B. He stiffened his body and threw his weight forward, in as much as he could, in hopes of rocking the chair hard enough to overcome gravity and send himself to the floor.

As the chair lurched forward, it caught the edge of the light roll-top desk, sending it toppling to the ground while his rocking chair remained steadfastly upright. Peter let out a low whistle of disbelief.

As a matter of principle, Peter did not curse. But at this moment, he let loose a string of obscenities before settling back into his chair, blank with the terror of it all.

He closed his eyes. *Think, Peter. Think*!

At the edge of the desk, something fluttered. A movement so slight that, had Peter even had his eyes open, he may not have seen it in the dim light.

Peter's eyes shot open at the cold chill of something tapping at his ankle. At first it registered as a simple itch. What a fine time to have an itch, he thought, and could not help but chuckle.

But the *tap-tapping*, that feeling of something soft and slightly... hairy... continued past his ankle, progressing up toward his knee.

Peter could not bring himself to look at the thing, now a mobile lump that undulated up the outside of his pant leg. He jerked the chair — *rock, jerk, rock, jerk* — inching it backward.

His eyes darted about the room, settling upon a similar shape that skittered into the dark corner of the room. It was one of Virginia's tarantulas.

"Help me, Peter!"

Anne's cries and the clawing pants-spider competed for his attention, but strangely it was his sister's words that ran to the forefront of his mind.

He remembered her saying, as they'd approached the decidedly spooky specter of Merrye House, that there was no such thing as ghosts, and no reason to worry.

* * *

Bruno tapped the brakes and threw the limousine into park. He exited the auto with a care and slowness born of great care for the fragile cargo onboard. As he circled his own vehicle, he noted with both surprise and sadness that Emily's car was parked alongside him.

"Oh, no. Not them, too!" Bruno shook his head as he moved to open the rear door. "Ah, well. What must be… must be."

With great effort, he pulled the large suitcase from the carriage and lugged it up the porch stairs. He was forced to stop a few times along the way; the baggage was not only heavy, but had to be handled with caution.

When Bruno stumbled upon a loose step — he'd been meaning to get to that — he nearly threw himself forward to protect the bag from hitting the ground.

He lurched into the house with his great baggage, calling out for Virginia and Elizabeth. In reply, he heard not them, but a woman's cries!

"Peter! Help! Aaaaaaah!"

Oh no, Bruno though, for he knew all too well the kind of trouble the children must have gotten up to.

* * *

In the drawing room above, Peter rocked his chair back and forth, inching his way across the room. His rocking had taken on even greater urgency, spurred by Bruno's arrival.

He'd let out a great gulping breath of relief at the sound of the door latches and locks sliding open. "Hello!" he screamed, certain that he was moments away from being released from his imprisonment.

A tarantula had made its way up Peter's pant leg. He willed himself to breathe — he was *fairly certain* that this type of spider did not bite. But the tiny prickles of its ascent toward his nether regions sent a cold chill crawling through him.

He was in this state when he called out to Bruno, who having entered the home, was dashing by the doorway when he saw Peter, who noted the suitcases in his hand. Bruno paused, his eyes meeting Peter's momentarily.

"Bruno! Thank goodness you're here! Can you please help me out? I..."

Bruno listed to one side, as if contemplating dropping one of the suitcases. But then... his eyes darted from Peter toward the cellar door and back and ultimately, he re-situated his suitcase, shook his head sadly, and continued on his way.

Peter, who had been doing his level best to remain calm until this moment, lost all semblance of cool. He rocked the chair wildly, screaming and thrashing, not understanding why Bruno wouldn't stop. *Why wouldn't he help me?*

All this led him to wondering if perhaps Emily was right and he'd been too charitable with his appraisement of them as harmlessly odd. *Why, they might be capable of anything!*

Something about those suitcases alarmed Peter, though he could not have articulated what it was. Maybe it wasn't the suitcases after all... maybe it was Bruno's manner. That sad, resigned nod.

All of these thoughts tumbled through Peter's mind in the space of mere seconds and the only conclusion he came to in the end was that it meant *trouble*.

Peter cried out a few more times, hoping that Bruno would return. When he heard the sound of the cellar door closing, a terrible finality, he redoubled his efforts to reach the desk with its letter opener.

Unable to twist his head to cart his path, he did not notice that his direction had shifted and that he was headed in the direction of the dumbwaiter shaft.

* * *

Elizabeth pulled her hand back, clutching it to her chest in shock, unable to conceive that a "pretty woman" like Anne would have bit her like a little dog! She examined the shallow wound, lapping at the blood that oozed from it.

Anne took the opportunity to jump up off the drainboard but Elizabeth, who had had just about enough of her, spun on heel and with one decisive motion, elbowed Anne in the forehead, sending the back of her head crashing to the metal drainboard below.

Elizabeth ran to Ralph's aid, crying, "Virginia! Help us!"

Virginia did not jump into the fray, but kept her sidelines cheerleading position. She clapped and cheered, offering little more than an occasional limp kick to help Ralph.

With a mighty lunge, Elizabeth threw herself upon Emily, wrestling her away. The movement disengaged her fingers from Ralph's eye sockets. She shrieked, the satisfaction of fulfilled vengeance.

Ralph threw his own palms to his eyes, a stream of gelatinous gore sliding through his fingers.

Emily tottered backwards, laughing and shrieking, a primal keening sound as she examined her gore-soaked fingers. She licked and nibbled at the mess, delirious with ecstasy, her body — rendered oddly stiff — teetering at the edge of the pit from which Uncle Ned's hoary hands reached up, clawing and grasping for Emily's slender ankles.

Emily's breath caught in her throat, the thud-thudding of her heart echoing like a drumbeat through every cell of her body.

All at once, Uncle Ned's hands found purchase in her calves, pulling Emily downward with one swift jerk. Her body landed with a soft thud, one leg cocked off-kilter, bent up such that her heel touched her lower back.

She did not scream. There was not enough breath left in her. Instead, she closed her fluttering eyelids to blind herself as the snarling, jackal-like humans descended upon her with their filth-coated, hairy coats and ragged claws.

Uncle Ned cried out, a sound that passed for delight. He shuffled off to a corner with his hands cupped around a secret treasure. In his palm, he held one of Emily's bright blue eyeballs.

The short-lived sound of Emily's undoing below was drowned out by the sounds of Ralph's agony above. Rendered blind, he thrashed about the floor like a great, giggled frog, his body undulating, slamming into the various items that littered the floor.

One of Ralph's frustrated kicks threw a coffin forward, tumbling into the pit. It landed with a crack, setting off another round of ungodly snarling and cries from below.

"Children!"

Chapter Twenty-Nine

The siblings quieted, spinning on heel toward the top of the stairs, where Bruno stood, silhouetted by the bright light of the room above, a heavy suitcase hanging from each hand.

The children lowered their heads, shame-faced. Ralph dropped his hands, revealing the half-filled pits of his mutilated eyes.

Bruno steadied himself and turned to close the cellar door behind him, lowering a bar across it. He descended the stairs to survey the scene, gingerly placing the battered suitcases side-by-side on the floor.

When he reached the edge of the pit, a quick downward glance at the flesh that littered the floor set his stomach to churning. He could hear the animals, who had scattered to the corners to pick apart their chosen Emily bits.

Bruno turned, first to Ralph, then to Elizabeth, who pointed down into the pit, crying, "That lady hurt Ralph! We had to do it!"

Bruno only nodded in reply for, strangely, in that moment, the calm of his conviction descended upon him. The sight of the basement with its splintered coffins, the blood-specked washboard and the snarling creatures in the pit below only served to bolster his courage in what he knew he must do.

No matter what.

Bruno patted each of the children on the head, pausing to sigh at the state of Ralph's eyes. "It's all right, Ralph. You'll be better soon." By way of reply, Ralph stuck his thumb deep in his mouth to quiet his moaning.

"Children, I've brought that nice surprise that I promised!"

"What is it? What is it?" Elizabeth and Virginia squealed, fairly quivering with anticipation.

Bruno gave a wry smile. The girls, even in their current state of ragged bloody dress, brought forth from him a surge of fatherly, protective love.

"Let me see!" Virginia cried.

Bruno waved the children over to him and sat himself upon one of the overturned coffins. They sank to their knees to sit before him and he motioned them still closer, lowering his voice to a conspiratorial whisper.

"Ahhh!" he said. "It's a secret surprise."

Bruno waved his hands at the nearby suitcases and scooted one toward him. Elizabeth and Virginia clapped their hands together in delighted anticipation. Ralph tilted his head as if to find his vision. He pulled out his thumb, his voice a liquid gagging sound.

The children watched Bruno undo first one latch, then the other, and open the suitcase.

Multiple, bound bundles of muted red dynamite sticks and fuses.

In the basement, Bruno smiled up into the light of the cellar door. It was a bit of cold comfort to know that the couple would make it out of the house after all.

In the pit behind them, Uncle Ned had turned the discarded coffin up on its end to fashion a sort of ladder out of the darkness.

The sound of the dynamite fuse increased as the fuse burned

down to its last half inch. Elizabeth and Virginia leaned in closer. Bruno noted with sadness that Ralph had gone silent on the floor, his arms wrapped about him in a fetal position. He had not intended that the children's ends would be painful. It was precisely what he'd hoped to avoid.

Elizabeth reached out to touch the burning fuse. Bruno gently guided her hand away.

"What is it going to do, Bruno?" she asked.

Bruno gulped. It was the first time that he had truly faced the physical reality of the convenient ending he held in his hands. He'd seen all manner of things in the war, after all. He pushed those thoughts — the memories of the missing-pieces men, the screaming wounded — away, tucking them into the darkest corners of his gray matter.

No, he thought. *This will be fast. There's enough dynamite here to blow up three Merrye Houses!* "Well," Bruno said. "It's going to make a big flash and go bang!"

"Oh, boy!" Virginia exclaimed.

Bruno turned the sticks of dynamite over in his hand, allowing the children to rub their palms along its surface. "Now, you see, children… this toy does something wonderful. Watch."

Ralph buried his head in his hands while Virginia and Elizabeth pulled themself closer to Bruno, watching him pull out a box of matches.

"What are you going to do with that, Bruno?" Elizabeth called out, breathless with anticipation.

Elizabeth's query, her trusting eyes focused on the matchbox clutched in his coarse hands, was enough to nearly melt Bruno's resolve. But he squeezed his eyes shut, summoning the image of his dear friend, Titus, to whom he'd made that promise many years ago.

When he opened his eyes again, he motioned to the girls to come into his embrace. He kissed each one of them on the top of the head and, shaking off any last vestiges of doubt, lit a match.

"Now, watch!"

Bruno touched the flame to the fuse, which burned with brilliant coruscation. The girls oohed and aahed at the yellow and red dance of the fire as it burned its way down the long fuse.

Bruno set the bundle back down in his lap and settled in, resting his feet on the open suitcase set before him.

* * *

Peter rocked the chair backward and it scooted back several inches. His abs and his arms ached with the effort but knowing that he had no time to waste, he gave himself one huge heave-ho. His entire weight shifted backward but, to his shock, he did not feel the expected thud of the floor rising to meet the rocker. Instead he tilted back, further still, as he tipped himself headfirst into the dumbwaiter shaft.

Bruno startled, his head whipping around toward the dumbwaiter shaft where Peter's figure had dropped, head first in the scattered wreckage of the rocking chair.

Peter shook his head as if to clear it. His uncertainty about the sequence of events quickly gave way to fear when he spotted the crackling flame in Bruno's lap.

Bruno's eyes darted from Peter, back to the dynamite. His face screwed up in confusion, as if he too were noticing the pack of lit dynamite situated in his lap. He made a futile try at snuffing out the flame, dabbing it with his shirt sleeve, before resigning with a shrug.

"Mr. Howe," he said calmly, "I'm not going to ask you how you got into this situation…"

Elizabeth and Virginia had lost all interest in Peter, their bright eyes trained on the sparkling toy.

Bruno continued. "But may I suggest, sir, that you leave the premises as quickly as possible?"

Peter wriggled and grasped at the lacy fabric that bound his wrists, pulling himself to an upright sitting position. As he broke free of the last vestiges of the chair, the panic that had been sitting in the pit of his stomach lurched up at him.

He scanned the room, crying out. "Anne! Anne! Where is she?!" He rose from the wreckage, casting off the last shreds of Virginia's spiderweb. He bolted for the stairs just as Anne's limp arm rose from the open coffin where she'd fallen.

"Anne!" Peter exclaimed, further rousing her from her half-conscious state.

Bruno watched the entire series of bizarre events with detachment. The world spun around him, everything seemingly far beyond his control. *Except for this*, he thought, rubbing his palm back and forth across the dynamite stick.

Peter grabbed onto Anne, draping her slowly awakening body across his back as he made for the stairs. It was tough going, evading the obstacles in his path with Anne hanging as dead weight about his neck.

Bruno stared down the fuse, its flame inching ever closer to the source. Without lifting his head, he called out to Peter once more. "Sir, I'd hurry if I were you..."

"I am hurrying, dammit!" Peter cried as he fumbled his way up the stairs. Anne had, thankfully, regained some control of herself and was half-limping along by Peter's side, the rickety stairway bending and swaying with the unexpected weight of two.

When they reached the top step, Anne held tight to the rail while Peter lifted the bar lock. Together he and Anne pushed through the cellar door, dragging themselves through the dining room.

* * *

The girls were the first to notice Uncle Ned's appearance. Elizabeth watched as first his hand, then the top of his head, breached the edge of the pit.

"Lookie!" she cried, pointing at him.

Virginia jumped up, smiling widely. "It's Uncle Ned!"

Behind Ned, Aunt Clara followed suit, dragging her scrap-bedecked body up the coffin ladder to join him. The slathering pair snarled, their arms raised high, hands curled into talons.

They rushed forward toward the girls, who shrank back.

* * *

Peter and Anne burst through the front door of the house, dragging themselves down the steps and through the yard, zigzagging this way and that, delirious with the desire to escape this dreaded place.

A brilliant flash of light hit them the millisecond before the THUDDING boom of the massive explosion behind them. The force of the blast threw them to the ground. Peter and Anne turned their faces toward each other, curling their arms about their heads to shield themselves.

Household objects and scraps of lumber rained down on them, landing amongst the weeds and the wet fungi. Here, a mounted bird. There, a chair leg. A silver platter.

And near Peter's hand… Virginia's wooden spider box.

Chapter Thirty

Ten Years Later

Peter closed the book, giving the camera what he imagined as a thoughtful pose. He uncrossed his legs and leaned forward.

"And so… the Merrye Syndrome was extinguished forever, with the family that carried it," he said. "Since my own branch of the family was rather distant, we never suffered that, uh, curse."

Peter laid the heavy tome on the table, beside the photo of his doe eyed daughter, Jessica.

"Yes, the whole things was an amazing experience to be sure. But for me at least, much good came of it. Being the only survivor, I inherited the Merrye's wealth, an amount that while not vast, was nonetheless an unexpected windfall. But even more important than that, my wife and… daughter. Without this experience, I would not have them."

Peter smiled, a bit awkward, and jumped forward to shut off the camera. He ran his hands through his hair, quite pleased with himself. *Yes*, he thought. *Such a strange experience. It will make a terrific documentary.*

While grateful for the opportunities it had presented to him, not the least of which were his lovely wife and daughter, he hoped that the film would close out this chapter of his life. He and Anne had discussed, many times, what it would be like to be free of the weight of that fateful day.

Peter tucked the memory away and dashed from the room, excited to share his experience with Anne. He closed the door, leaving the empty room, with its oversized picture window, behind him.

Through that window, and across the garden, Peter and Anne's daughter, Jessica, played. A ditsy floral printed dress nearly dwarfed the girl's slight frame. She was bent over, as if planting a flower, perhaps, or examining something of great interest.

Her body jerked with the startle of excitement and the girl rose up onto all fours, her limbs splayed out to the side. She crawled like that, low to the ground, her eyes trained on a cricket. She sprung forward, her head dipping down to the blade of grass where the creature rested.

The girl watched, for a moment, her eyes inches from the crickets. She examined its movements, its legs bent at awkward angles, and then — suddenly — lurched forward, mouth wide open, to snatch the insect with the tip of her tongue.

Jessica ground her teeth, chewing slowly to better enjoy the feel of the cricket's parts as they rolled about the cavern of her mouth. She swallowed and sat back, a low crouch, and felt around her mouth with her tongue, searching for any errant insect parts.

Jessica enjoyed playing games with her parents. The trio had often joked that they were like the Three Musketeers — always together. But for all their good nature, she knew that her parents did not ever want to play her favorite game; they had, in fact, told her in no uncertain terms that not only would they not play it, but that she was not to either.

But sometimes, in the afternoons, while her parents napped, or her father worked on his writing, Jessica would find herself alone in the garden. And on those days, with the scent of summer hanging in the air, it felt as if the insects called to her.

On a perfect day like that, when she was quite certain that she was alone, she would crouch down in the grass to play…

Spider.

Deleted Scenes

Prologue
1977

Spider Baby is a film that lives in the seams. It's stitched together with love, black humor, and whatever film stock Jack Hill could lay hands on that week. That's part of the charm. And part of the reason why this scene, written by Dayna Noffke for the novelization, never made it into the final version of this book.

This moment was Dayna's way of expanding the mythology. Of imagining what might've been happening outside the frame. It gives us a glimpse into the domestic, slightly warped heart of Peter and Anne, characters who exist in the margins of the Spider Baby. Here, (as well as in the epilogue) they are granted their own little chamber piece: a man with a pipe and a dream, a woman trying to remain supportive but skeptical, and a daughter whose subtle behavioral shifts suggest that something's very wrong beneath the surface.

Though we chose to omit it from the main narrative for reasons of tone and pacing, we couldn't bear to let it vanish entirely. So we're including it here, not as an outtake, but as a bonus reel—a glimpse behind the curtain of what could have been, written by someone who deeply understands this world.

Enjoy this deleted scene for what it is: a love letter to Peter, Anne, and the weirdly tender heart of Spider Baby.

* * *

"For the last time, Anne! It's *not* a porno!" Peter said, as he screwed the shiny-new 16mm Bell and Howell camera to its tripod.

"Oh, Peter. I'm kidding for cripe's sake! You should work on your sense of humor," she replied. Peter knew she wasn't serious, *of course*, but his nerves were strung extra taut that day, an unspoken uneasiness having descended over their house in the past few weeks.

Though neither, if asked, could have pinpointed the wellspring of this feeling of, whatever it was seemed to have latched onto their young daughter, Jessica, who had, quite suddenly lost all interest in her friends, and in the girlish preoccupations that had formerly held sway over her. Of late, they'd noticed her staring out windows at all hours of the day and night.

Peter had come upon her picking through the grass and plucking out an insect, which she held to her face, examining the soft space that was the meeting of exoskeleton and pincers.

He had thought it a bit strange, as it certainly wasn't typical of Jessica to handle bugs, but he'd promptly written off his misgivings as a sort of latent misogyny after Anne reminded him that "lots of boys like to play with bugs!"

Anne had gone so far as to proudly predict Jessica's future profession of scientist. Peter nodded in agreement, holding his own thoughts on the matter tight to his chest. But a few days later, when Anne had happened upon Jessica's game of dolls, as she stood in the doorway, watching in the wistful way of a proud parent, she was alarmed to see Jessica stripping her dolls of their clothing before tying them to chairs with lengths of brightly-colored yarn.

Anne, not knowing what to do, had walked away in stunned silence. When she brought the matter up with Peter later that night, she soft-stepped around it, once more downplaying the seriousness of what she had seen.

Peter, to his credit, could see through Anne in that moment and did not pull the "I told you so" card, insisting instead that the girl should see a doctor. It was a position from which he could not be swayed, though the discussion had been temporarily tabled in the interest of marital peace.

Now Peter stood at a mirror, taking a last swipe at his Vitalis-infused side part. He tucked his pocket comb away in a side drawer and turned to his *so-very-blond* wife, to reveal his full figure, decked out in a velvet smoking jacket, silken pajama pants and slippers. "You don't think it's too much?" he asked.

Peter had waffled, spending far more time than he'd care to admit thinking about it. He'd stared into the mirror, talking himself up. Despite having settled on the outfit, because - after all - *it was just the sort of thing a director would wear* - he still felt the entire getup a bit silly. It was a clear put-on.

Anne studied him, her reflection shifting in the mirror. Peter knew that, for better or worse, she could, without exception, be depended upon to offer her honest opinion. She approached her husband to place a gentle hand on his jacket collar, smoothing an invisible crease.

"I think you look wonderful, dear. But, Peter… I still think that… it's a lot, isn't it? Making an entire film by yourself?"

Peter might have been exasperated by the question had he not been wondering the same thing. He knew well the subtext of her query, knew that he had messed up and that he should have taken *those damn movie people* up on the offer to buy their story all those years ago when, despite his lawyer's pleading, he turned them all down cold, insistent that if he just held out…

Despite dismissing the lack of forthcoming offers with a flip *no use crying over spilt milk*, Peter's head ached with regret anew each time he recalled that following week, the excruciating ache of sweating by the phone, waiting for the offer that never came.

Anne had been gracious at the time and the two of them had long since unhitched their wagon from the idea of Hollywood and settled, if not happily, at least contentedly, into suburban life. On those rare occasions, perhaps the summer barbecue, where conversation turned to the subject of Peter and Anne's erstwhile Hollywood adventures, Peter's pat dismissal of, "Just out here living my tertiary dream" was always good for a chuckle.

Anne was glad to be rid of the prospect, happy to sally forth with their extraordinarily ordinary lives. That is, until the afternoon that Peter got a wild hair that led he and Anne to a matinee showing of *The Exorcist.*

"That was a true story, Anne! Just like ours! Why, I'd say our story - the Merrye story - is even wilder than that one."

Anne had nodded noncommittally, not wanting to encourage him. But the wild hair had taken root. Peter brought it up often enough that Anne commented more than once that Peter was *positively obsessed!* Two years of failed pitches later, Peter burst into the kitchen to declare that he would, "make the movie myself, by God!"

At first, Anne was firmly in his corner. After all, the couple had spent what seemed like half their courtship at the drive-in, taking in the blood and guts masterpieces of Roger Corman and ilk. But Anne's enthusiasm cooled as the realities of producing a project came to bear, and she began to insist that since *they were parents now*, their money should be shuffled off into Treasury Bonds or some-such. Peter responded they might as well go ahead and purchase their tombstones in advance for good measure.

All of that to arrive at this moment, where they stood in Peter's office-come-movie-studio with its new-to-them leatherette side chair and a mishmashed assortment of blinding Tungsten lights - Peter's idea, an impulse purchase from a rental house going-out-of-business sale.

He justified his purchases by repeatedly pointing out how

much money he saved by *buying used*, while in truth he had more than spent those savings with his insistence upon buying a shiny new Bell and Howell 16mm camera.

"Peter?" Anne tapped Peter's shoulder, urging him back to the present with a reassuring smile. His permanently-furrowed brow loosened a hair and Anne wrapped her arms around him. "I'm sure you'll be a great…"

"Narrator. I'm the narrator," Peter filled in the blank. "This is just a teaser. A prelude to get investors interested in the story again. Chum the waters, so to say."

Anne nodded. "Well, that sounds like a very… interesting idea." Peter clocked the *word interesting*, Anne-speak for ridiculous, but was too concerned with getting into character to fuss. He pecked Anne's cheek and walked her to the door. She let herself out with a perfunctory, "Good luck, Peter."

Luck? Who needs LUCK?! I've got a story, he thought, as he settled into the squeaky leather armchair that faced the camera. He cleared his throat.

"Peter Piper picked a peck of pickled peppers. Peter Piper pickled a peckl- oh, darn it." He contorted his mouth, slid his lower jaw from side to side and then opened wide, the shape of an O. He took his time, letting each word slide out at its own leisurely pace. "Peter Piper picked a… peck of… pickled… peppers." He slapped his knee in self-congratulation.

Peter adjusted himself, tilting his legs just so. He crossed them and picked up an oversized leather-bound volume which he balanced, first on his crossed legs - *No, no! Too casual* - and then in the palm of his wide open left hand.

He fiddled with the *oh-so-carefully chosen* props on the table beside him. First, he placed the unlit pipe at the corner of the table. He second-guessed that, instead holding it in his lip. He pulled the pipe out to swing it about, gesticulating in what he imagined was the way of a college professor.

When that didn't feel quite right somehow, he sipped from etched rocks glass of bourbon. Ultimately, he settled on leaving the props on the table, arranged at right angles beside a framed photo of himself with Anne and Jessica.

Peter looked directly into the camera, squinting at the curved reflection of his face in the lens before opening the book. He turned the pages - crisp, the binding of oiled leather scanned columns of text, his finger stopping to rest on the entry labeled MERRYE SYNDROME.

He cleared his throat, testing the sound of his own voice with variations of the words. "MErrye Syn-drome. MerrYE Syn-drum. Merrye."

He set the open book to the side. Realizing that he'd already been holed up in the stuffy office for the better part of an hour, he decided he'd might as well get on with it already.

Jump into the deep end, he thought, as he sprang up to hit the camera's shutter button. He settled back in the chair to the whir of the film passing the gate.

He had readied himself for his monologue, the opening meticulously crafted over the course of several months. It was strange to him that now, as his gaze turned to the mechanical eye, he grew nervous, the words he had not only memorized, but written himself, tumbling down the rabbit hole of his mind. He swiped the cuff of his shirt across his sweaty brow, his eyes locking on the camera's distorted view of him. One thought occurred and pushed all the others from the front of his brain: *My Lord! Is my forehead really that large?*

Peter rubbed his temples, urged by the thought of the magazine running through precious (and expensive) frames of film while he sat in that chair forgetting everything he'd taken such care to memorize. *Focus, Peter. Focus*, he urged himself.

He scanned his surroundings, settling upon the book, which he once more dropped into his back on his lap, which he commenced reading aloud.

"The Merrye Syndrome, so called because its only known occurrence is among the descendants of one Ebenezer Merrye.

A progressive age regression, beginning about the tenth year, and continuing steadily throughout the victim's lifetime."

" It is believed that eventually the victim of the Merrye Syndrome may even regress beyond the pre-natal level, reverting to a pre human condition of savagery and cannibalism. Many authorities do not accept the existence of the Merrye Syndrome."

Peter's delivery grew more confident, all slick sparkle and disturbingly-straight teeth. He spun the book to face the camera, the better to display the black and white carnival barker style photos, an attempt to sell titillation in the guise of science.

The pictured subjects were a lineup of nearly-nude wild men and women with elongated teeth, with limbs that jutted and bowed, and the blackest, saucer-sized pupils that floated inside sunken sockets.

Beneath the photos, a caption read, "Wild Men and Women, displayed by the J.R. Carnival Company as part of their Wonders of Human Nature sideshow."

Peter let the image linger only momentarily, recalling what he had read about showmanship and the importance of holding back, of giving the audience *just a little taste.*

He spun the book away from the camera and continued talking, his voice having settled into a smooth stream of rehearsed ballyhoo. He sped up his delivery, words crashing together in a race against the short remains of the whirring film reel.

"Horrible? Yes. Incredible? Yes! But true, nevertheless, as I know only too well. But, of course, there is no Merrye Syndrome anymore. No. It was extinguished forever on that fateful day ten years ago. The motion picture you are about to watch attempts to tell the tale of that day and the tragedy of Merrye Syndrome."

Peter sat back into his chair and closed the book with an air of great gravitas. Aiming his toothy grin at the camera, it occurred to him that he wasn't certain how to finish; but before he could, a flash of movement in the window grabbed his attention.

He turned toward it, watching - at first - with a father's proud eye, as his dark-haired daughter ran in circles around a perfectly manicured expanse of cyan green grass.

His smile dropped. Again, it occurred to him that her behavior seemed a bit... off...

The camera clicked, the perfectly timed end of the film magazine signaling him to stand, at which point all thoughts of his daughter's behavior vanished, replaced by the realization that he'd forgotten to say *"major* motion picture."

Ah, next time.

Chapter 1
The Messenger's Extended Journey

Before his brief but unforgettable appearance in Spider Baby, *Mantan Moreland had already established a complex and enduring legacy in American cinema. A beloved character actor throughout the 1940s and '50s, Moreland rose to prominence playing roles shaped by the era's racial stereotypes—often in the vein of Stepin Fetchit (Lincoln Perry) or Sleep 'n' Eat (Willie Best). He began his career in vaudeville and minstrel shows before finding stardom in Black-owned studio productions, navigating a treacherous industry with wit, timing, and undeniable charm.*

Between 1957 and 1964, however, Moreland became a casualty of Hollywood's ever-shifting moral compass. His style of comedy, once embraced, was now deemed offensive to Black audiences—though few of those audiences were actually consulted. As a result, Moreland found himself edged out of the industry and forced back onto the touring circuit at an age when such work was especially taxing.

The exact details of how Moreland came to be cast in Spider Baby *are hazy, but it's clear that director Jack Hill sought to offer him both work and recognition. The role served as a kind of stunt casting: placing a once-iconic comedian into a film where he would be violently killed in the opening moments. Additional scenes involving a secondary family unit were reportedly written specifically to give*

Moreland another day on set—something Hill had also done for Lon Chaney Jr., particularly during the more challenging days of Chaney's sobriety.

This scene, in as it exists in the book, was cut for pacing, and also for the fact that it only exists in the original film itself because Jack wanted to get Mantan Moreland another day's worth of pay. This is just one of the many reasons we love Jack Hill.

* * *

He gathered himself. Raised a hand to shield his eyes and scanned the mailbox numbers again, despite having already spent the last half hour cruising the rutted side street. He noted, not without irritation, that he'd drawn the rapt attention of a squirrelly little kid who had taken up position at the edge of his unkempt front yard to examine him through the picket fence slats.

Between the bug-eyed kid, his temperamental bike and the heat wave, he was tempted to call it a day, forgo his delivery fee in favor of getting home to the bottle of cola, *the last one in his fridge*, he recalled.

Still, that damn envelope — that and the looming specter of the any-day-now "rent's late" knock from his landlord — taunted him.

So he threw the pasty kid a perfunctory wave and called out. "Scuse me!" The boy did not return the gesture, in fact, didn't acknowledge him at all, just kept right on staring while he twisted a broken stick in the dirt. The boy looked up, the messenger jumped at the sound of the storm door. It flung open to deposit a little girl — *dammit if she isn't holding a cold cola bottle in her scabby little kid paws* — into the yard.

The messenger tried again. "Scuse me! Do you know where the Merrye Residence is?" He waved his arms over his head, then grudgingly cut his ignition to address them again.

"I said Merrye Residence! Can y'all tell me where to find the

Merrye House?" The kids froze up, a silent tableau, and the messenger realized that he'd forgotten it was no longer necessary to shout.

The door to the clapboard house opened. A skinny mother in a flowered housecoat and curlers flew out, shooing the kids back to the house. She ushered them inside and then trotted to the fence. The messenger knew this *"there's a black man in my yard"* look. He painted on his best, "yes ma'am," smile as the woman leaned her ample top half over the points of her fence.

She cut him off before he could get a word out. "Can I help you?"

"Well, *yes ma'am*. I'm looking for the Merrye Residence." The woman gasped, a nervous reflex. Her hands flew to her cheeks and she turned heel to push the children into the safety of her sagging front porch. "No. No, sir. If there is any such place, we don't know anything about it."

The mother slammed the door shut. *Well, goddamn woman. I must be scarier than I thought.* The messenger had opened his mouth to speak — though he wasn't sure exactly what he'd have said — but the words stuck in the cage of his parched throat. It didn't matter.

Experience had taught him that there was no talking to some people; no matter how polite he might be. He pushed back his visored cap to scratch his curly white-thatched scalp and gave the woman a little nod before settling back into his seat. After a few false starts, the motor cranked back to stammering life under the family's suspicious curtain-shrouded faces.

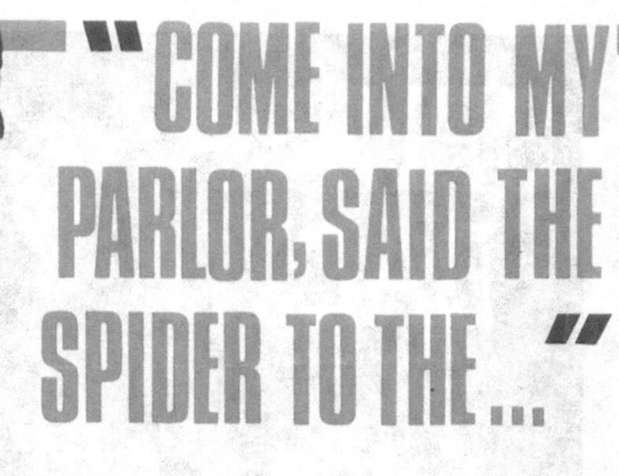
"COME INTO MY PARLOR, SAID THE SPIDER TO THE ..."

SEDUCTIVE INNOCENCE of LOLITA
SAVAGE HUNGER of a BLACK WIDOW!

AMERICAN GENERAL
Presents

WHAT EVER HAPPENED TO....
SPIDER BABY

STARRING
SPIDER BABY
AND LON CHANEY

SPIDER
BABY
A FILM BY JACK HILL

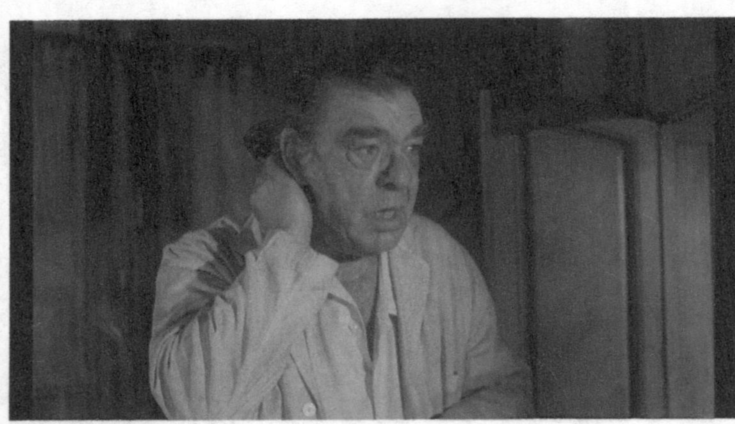

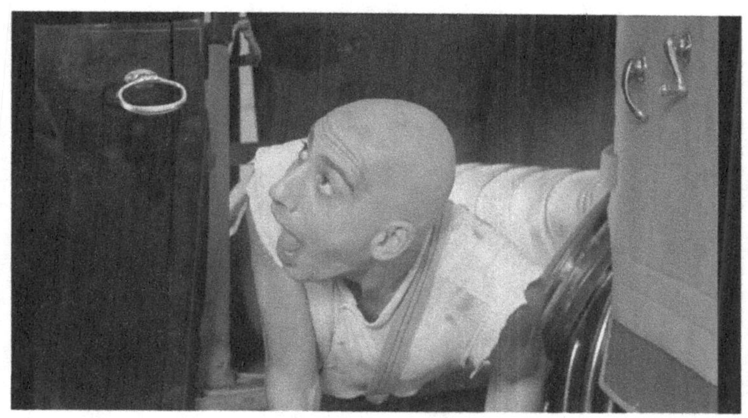

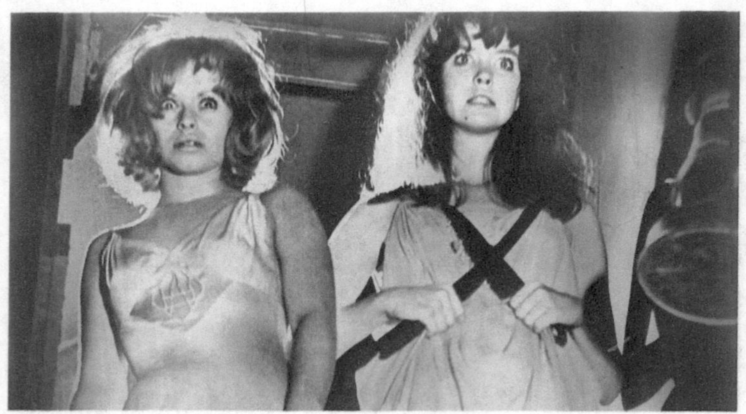